KU-310-921

For Harriet and Toby,
Diana and I will be riding
beside you, always . . .

1

Charlie Crow

I killed my first man in the springtime of nearly thirty years ago. Shot him dead more by accident than design. I was on my way riding north to Montana from the Big Bend country in West Texas, leaving behind me the memory of Hannah Dubois sitting on the stoop of her two by four outfit and Sam Dubois, her dead husband, face down in a nameless grave at the back of their run down barn.

Close by the Arizona line, I signed on for the spring round up at the Lazy Bee and befriended Harry Boyd, young, handsome Harry Boyd from Carol Creek Texas, a red-headed, fiery Irishman who was also heading north and getting work where he could find it. We were of the same age, eighteen, and we cottoned to each other from the get go, rode nighthawk together on many occasions. He had a sweet baritone voice and you could be assured the cattle would not spook when Harry Boyd was singing his Irish ballads. Evenings when not working the cattle we spent nursing our beers in McCoy's Sundance Bar, Merritsburg's only saloon, or chatting to the Mexican waitress, Juanita, over apple pie and cream in the local diner.

Jerry McCoy kept a large, caged green parrot behind the bar and when the saloon keeper was not around, customers delighted in trying to teach the big bird cuss words and enjoying the man's irritation when it successfully levelled those same words in the direction of the suited, after morning church, Sunday customers.

Harry Boyd fancied his chances with Juanita although she seemed to have little interest in Harry, the local cowhands or, seemingly, men in particular. Harry got a little possessive even though she gave him no cause to think that she was interested in him, not even when he sang for free to entertain her appreciative customers on a Saturday night.

On the Saturday of the gunfight, I was leaning on the polished bar top trying to make a quirly out of the dust at the bottom of Durham sack and my one beer last the evening, when Harry burst through the swing doors and called me out. He yelled across the room at me, red-faced, accusing me of sparking Juanita behind his back and saying for sure he was going to kill me. He had been drinking cheap booze or mescal available from the bars on the Mex side of town, spending the money given to him by the appreciative music lovers in the diner. It took me by surprise and even more so when he unlimbered his sidearm and fired two rounds in my direction. The first bullet hit the parrot, blowing it into a cloud of green feathers; the second bounced off the hardwood bar and took the beaver top hat clean off the mayor's head, causing both him and his domino playing companion to hit the sawdust covered floor.

Like most cowhands I carried a gun, an old thumb breaking .38 Navy Colt conversion I had won in a poker game, using it for rattlers or for putting down injured or sick animals — not for shooting people. I wore it in a scuffed brown leather holster on a plain leather belt which, lacking shell loops, necessitated me carrying a couple of loose rounds in my vest pocket, rounds I never needed as rattlesnakes were in fact best avoided, and a habit I still have to this day.

I never drew that pistol for anything other than work but when I saw Harry lining up his Colt on me straight armed, I pulled the piece and fired in his general direction even as I was diving for the floor alongside of the frightened mayor. My first shot broke a lamp and the second hit Harry just above his right eye, the heavy slug taking out the back of his head and spreading it across the wall above the black potbellied stove. He staggered backwards, a look of surprise on his young face, a look I have seen many times since, a look that has always given me concern. Why the surprise? If you are in a gunfight, chances are you or someone else is going to get hurt.

My ears were ringing from the concussion of the rounds in the confined space of the saloon. The black powder smoke that enveloped the room burned my eyes, making them water, or was I crying for what had just happened to both Harry Boyd and to me? Harry was dead and I was lost to a life I never really wanted or ever dreamed of having.

They sold Harry's guitar, his gun-belt, his horse and saddle and fined his corpse the exact amount raised from their sale which McCoy said would pay for a new bird and for the mayor's new stove pipe hat. They also fined me $10, a quarter of my month's wages, to pay for the lamp and Harry's burying, making it known to me in the process that even though it was clearly a case of self-defence, I was not welcome in Merritsburg. I drew what was left of my pay and continued on my journey north to Montana.

I still see Harry Boyd at night when the darkness is upon me, that look of anguish on his face as he pulled the trigger of his handgun, and I hear the sweet notes he sang to the longhorns under the moonlit Arizona sky. I still hear the squawk of McCoy's green parrot and sometimes when it snows, I fancy I see the green of its feathers fluttering amid the white snowflakes.

But that was nearly thirty years ago and there had been a lot of surprised facial expressions and wide-eyed disbelief since then.

2

Billy Joe Watts

'You're the new man, I guess. What's your name?'

'Crow,' I said, 'Charlie Crow.'

'Have I heard of you from somewhere?'

'I don't know, have you?'

'What do they call you, Charlie?'

'Mostly they call me Old Timer.'

He studied me for a moment or two, thinking, and said, 'I can see why they would do that. Long in the tooth for this game, aren't you?'

I shrugged.

'What should I call you?'

'Whatever your preference is but Crow is good.'

'OK then, Crow, you hightail it up to that knoll where the dead oak sits and take that Winchester of yours and you

7

fire two shots in the direction of anyone who rides up the gulley. They don't stop, put them down, horse or rider. I don't care much which so long as they keep out of our way.'

I nodded and stared at him a moment before saying, 'It's a Marlin.'

'Excuse me?' he said, a puzzled look furrowing his brow.

'My carbine, it's a Marlin.'

The puzzled, questioning look stretched to his pale eyes.

'My saddle gun, it's a Marlin, not a Winchester.'

He was chewing his lip, thinking, studying me some more. 'Whatever, just so long as it shoots straight, I don't give a crap what it is.'

He handed me a pair of army field glasses then turned away and walked back down the wash to where the crew were branding a small herd of fat, probably tick infested, definitely stolen, Mexican cattle.

Taking the Marlin from the saddle scabbard and shouldering my canteen, I climbed up to the ridge and settled myself on a rock from which I could clearly see down and into the long gulley. It was a hot, sun-drenched day and the flat rock was sun-baked hot. A hot backside and a hat the inside of which was hotter than an oven.

Why and how had I come to this? I guessed the five bills a day with twenty up front was incentive enough to a hungry man.

I shook some rolling tobacco from the Durham sack and rolled a couple of smokes, setting one beside me and, pulling the sack's tab closed with my teeth, I fired the other quirly with a blue topped match and settled back against the grey granite rock.

An hour or two and a brief sleep later, a lone rider on a paint horse rode into the gulley and approached the ridge and looked to be heading for the wash. He rode straight-backed with his head held high, eyes searching the ridge and the trail ahead of him. I levered a shell into the Marlin's smooth breach and put a round over his head. He stopped, paused then came on. I put another round closer this time but after only a slight falter he came on again faster and I could see a flash of metal on his vest, just over the heart. I looked at him through the glasses; a slight, slim man, dressed in black, thin, dark, moustachioed upper lip.

A lot of years have passed between me and Harry Boyd and the green parrot, and I am not in the killing business anymore; the days have long since gone when I would hire my gun and then cap a man for money. Sometimes hiding behind a badge, I was getting too old, too smart or too lazy, I am never sure which.

I sighted with care and dumped a round a couple of feet in front of the pony. It reared and turned but his owner brought it back under control. He still came on even though the animal was restless. I capped two more rounds in quick succession at the animal's front hoofs; it reared, dumping the rider on the ground and fled back the way it had come. The man seemed unperturbed. Getting to his feet, he picked up his dislodged hat, brushed off his pants, drew a handgun and fired several defiant straight armed rounds in my direction, all of which fell well short. He then holstered the piece, worked the long, drooping moustache with thumb and index finger, and stared up at the ridge for a long while before turning and following the frightened paint back up the gulley.

The afternoon dragged on and my canteen was bone dry of the warm, brackish water it had contained. Once a blue jay winged low over the grey granite hill and settled on a branch of the gnarled dead oak tree; he stayed only a minute before being chased off by a shining, coal black, squawking crow. The big bird rested a while, glanced my way and headed back down to the draw from where I could smell the burning of hide and hear the bawling cattle as the irons were applied.

Fresh food down there, a nut bucket maybe. Smart, those crows.

I settled back down on my hot rock and waited. Maybe an hour later, the paint and rider reappeared but this time there were over a dozen riders with him and they looked loaded for bear, and the stars glistened in the daylight. I scuttled back to my horse, sheathed the carbine and hightailed it down and out of there, skirted the wash where they were branding the stolen cattle and headed for Wyoming and hoped for an all-round cooler clime. I heard later that the man on the paint was Wally Dade, a feisty US Marshal and that there was a big gunfight along that ridge and down in the gulley and along the wash that day, and that several men, including my ex-employer, were killed. I wonder if he blamed me for not stopping the posse or whether he died wondering if a hundred, tick-infested Mex cattle were worthy of the dying.

It turned out that Wyoming was not

a good choice. I arrived in the middle of what later became known among other things as The Johnson County War, although some preferred the Powder River War. By whatever name it was known, it was a war, and the middle of a range war is not a good place to be, especially if you are broke. Sometimes it might pay off though, if you can see which side is winning and become a part of that winning side. It was a possibility but my gut told me it would be a long, confusing war and a lot of dying was likely. That's how it turned out but I did not stay to see the end of it; I knew how it would work out. It was not a new story. Big ranchers take on the little ranchers, the settlers, and set to wiping them out, and they damned near did, all of them. Only the intervention of the 6th US Cavalry really prevented a massacre and although responsible for many deaths, the suits and the money always win and, as far as I know, not one of the big ranchers was ever held accountable for the many killings, none of which I was part of.

That one wasn't my first rodeo, I had been on the losing side before and, to my shame, in Johnson County, I ended up on the side of the money. I joined up with a bunch of gunfighters, stone killers, imported gunmen and riff raff from below the Texas border country. They were hired at five bucks a day and a bonus of fifty for every nester they killed. I never earned a big fifty but I took my fives for as long as I could stand it then split back south; somehow I thought the air smelled cleaner there.

I palled up with a kid from Missouri by the name of Billy Joe Watts, another young, good-looking kid brighter than most. He reminded me a little of Harry Boyd; same temperament when he was sober — which was most of the time — but a little rowdy when the booze was in him. Unlike Harry, Billy was plenty fast with a handgun and carried a blued Colt .45 with a four and a half inch barrel, wearing the weapon low, as was the way with young pistoleros. He was good with both hands, not a commonplace thing. I taught him some moves and he kind of stuck by me, followed me around, looked in my direction for approval when he did stuff. I was flattered and when he asked if he could quit and ride out with me, I agreed. He would be good company, I thought; after all, it was a hell of a long ride back to the Big Bend country. We did have some fun money for the journey and, living off the land, stopping now and then for a brief while, taking on a quick riding job or swamping out a saloon for vitals and a drink, we got by. The good times did not last and we parted company when he shot and killed the farmer in a small town called Crystal just a little north of the Montana Wyoming border.

I didn't see it all but what I did see left me cold. I don't know how it started, I was taking a leak in the alleyway when it kicked off. Maybe just a joshing at the bar that one man or the other read wrong or took offence at, an easy thing to do, a stranger in a strange town, a few drinks, a ready tongue and it begins.

I was coming back through the swing doors when Billy Joe Watts drew his Colt and shot the farmer whose gun had not even really cleared the leather. That may possibly have been because he was not a gunman and Billy Joe was, and like I said, he was fast. Had the farmer been a slicker gun, he may well have put Billy down but that wasn't the way of it. Billy's bullet was not fatal and the man tried to get to his feet clutching his shoulder, blood seeping through his gnarled work-worn fingers. His hand was nowhere near his holstered gun when Billy capped him again, this time putting the ball through the man's left eye.

An unnecessary killshot as far as I could see and later I told him so, showed him clearly my disapproval. The town only had a part time constable as their lawman and he quickly accepted that it looked as if it was a self-defence shooting and the barkeep, who had seen the start of it but not the end of it as he ducked down behind the bar when the fracas began, said it looked that way to him. The constable took some notes, called the undertaker, shook Billy Joe Watts's hand and went back home to his wife, dog and warm bed.

Early the next morning, the day bleak and grey, I packed my bedroll in my poncho and hooked my war bag over the saddle horn of the bay horse that had carried me steadfastly from Wyoming. Billy Joe watched me from the door of the run down line shack we had roosted in for fourteen days while we worked cattle out of the draws for a local rancher who was shorthanded and offered us the two weeks' work.

'You going without me, Charlie?' He was leaning in the doorway, braces hanging down over his dirty undershirt, long blond hair rumpled and hiding one side of his face, he shook it back with an almost imperceptible nod of his head. There was an unmistakeable look of amusement on his narrow lips and a glint of anger in his pale blue eyes. Had he been wearing a gun I might have wondered how fast he really was when not up against a sodbuster, but he wasn't so it made no never mind.

'I'll draw my pay and ride south, Billy. Thanks for the company, some of it was fun.' I swung up on to the cold saddle and looked down at him but did not offer my hand.

'This because I killed the sodbuster, that why you are mad at me?'

'Not because you killed him, Billy, but the way in which you killed him. He was down and out, no threat to you, you didn't have to fire that second round, that killshot.'

'He could still have pulled on me.'

'Not in a million years, all he was thinking about was staying alive and he may well have done so had you not capped that round.'

'You've killed men . . . '

'Only when it was them or me and

that was not the case yesterday. You killed him because you have a mean streak in you, which you may grow out of and you may not, but either way I don't want to be around your mean-ness.'

'You scared of me, Charlie?' He smiled a cold smile, the kind of smile that sends the tiniest of shivers along a man's spine, just enough to irritate.

'I'm always wary around a natural born killer with a gun.'

'You judging me, Charlie? You riled because I shot a nester who was on the prod?'

'I'm no judge, kid, the only man who can judge you is you, that's the only judgement worth a damn out here. Know who you are, then live or die with that knowledge.'

'Billy the Kid, huh? You know that has a familiar ring to it.'

'A two bit gunslinger, five foot two of nothing, shot to death at the age of twenty-one by a two bit county sheriff? That what you aspire to being?'

'Aspire? What's aspire?'

'Forget it, be seeing you around, Billy.' I turned the bay.

'You can bet on that, Old Timer; sometime, someday somewhere further down the line.'

That chill again, that dark feeling that I would be seeing him again somewhere down the trail but hoping not.

3

Laura Bainbridge

Over the next four days, the big bay and I put a lot of country between us and the young killer Billy Joe Watts but even so, it did not seem to be far enough. There was something dead and cold in those blue eyes as I recalled those last smiling words, a smile which did not stray beyond his thin lips. I rode hard and long but the bay was up to it and by nightfall on the fifth day, we finally cleared the state of Montana, leaving behind the misery of Johnson County and the bloody range war that would continue for weeks to come.

With the Big Horn Mountains on my left, it was my intention to cut east and into the Dakota Territories but with a cold breeze and a wisp of snow on the wind, I decided to stick to the foothills and make camp among the lodge pole pines growing there if I could find a sheltered spot that would offer some water and grass for the tired bay. I found better than that, though.

In a sheltered clearing, we stumbled upon a run down cabin which I took to be a line shack of sorts, with an adjoining lean-to and a cold water well. The place was deserted and draughty but better than sleeping under a tarp. There were no recent signs of life except the distinct smell of cat and large spoors in the mud around the well. Too high up and too cold I reasoned for snakes, but I checked anyway and disturbed a nest of pack rats, the residents of which I shooed out into the cold night, wishing them well.

There was a serviceable bunk and a potbellied stove which, after caring for my horse and settling him in the lean-to, I lit with kindling and logs stacked by its side, the open front sending a warm glow into the cabin's single room. I fried the last of the bacon in my skillet and with the last of the bread I had purchased from a rotund rancher's wife two days earlier. I ate well, and took a swig from the jug I had bought from the lady's husband after sampling it with him in the barn where he kindly fed the bay.

I could have lingered but felt I had to be moving on while the weather held. My rough map told me that somewhere a few miles to the west of me was the small township of Cheyenne Wells. The next morning, after a cup of hot Joe and clean-up with water from the well heated on the stove, I made my way toward it.

Cheyenne Wells was small by any comparison; two false fronted rows of clapboard buildings substantial enough but in need of a lick of paint and a hammered nail here and there, ran the length of the rutted main street. A shuttered saloon, several stable dwellings and a large general store cum saloon cum boarding house that offered just about anything from a haircut and shave, bath, range clothes and ammunition to dentistry. I wondered who would be hard pressed enough to use the latter and guessed if that was the only game in town and for miles around, a few moments of pain was a whole lot better than nursing a sick tooth. It was the only building that showed a dim but welcoming light.

I hitched the bay to the sagging rail and climbed on to the raised, boarded sidewalk and entered the store. The interior of the building was dark, a darkness relieved only by the faint light offered by the flickering oil lamp I had seen from the street and the leaden, snow filled sky glinting with a flurry of sparkling snowflakes. The only other person in the store apart from the stocky, red-faced, grey-aproned store-keeper sitting behind the counter was a grey-haired woman dressed from neck to ankles in a long grey duster who studied me some before returning her attention to a bolt of material she was fondling.

The storekeeper seemed pleased to see me and I guessed that was more for the break in the monotony of the customer free morning as it was for the expectation that I might spend some money. He folded the newspaper and gave me his full attention.

'Morning,' he said. 'Not a good one but we are still here and breathing and that is something to be thankful for.' He smiled at his own wisdom, offered me his cold hand. 'Mort Jennings, I own the place. Haircut or a shave or a pulled tooth, I'm your man. The bath, well, you're on your own there,' he chortled. 'Coffee? You look about done in.'

I took the outstretched hand. 'Crow, Charlie Crow.'

'Take a load off, Charlie. The stove is fired up, open the front wide. I'll put the Joe on. You want a coffee?' he called to the woman.

She nodded. 'Thanks, Mort, I could use one sure enough.' She had a rasping but not unpleasant voice.

She smiled at me and nodded before

returning her attention to the cloth and for the first time, I noticed as she turned that she was carrying a short Winchester pump action shotgun close to the hip. I wondered about that; it was a very new weapon only recently available in any number.

'Anything I can get you while the coffee boils?' Mort asked.

'I could use a warm jacket and some supplies but mostly I would like some information.'

'About?'

'There's a line shack, looks abandoned, about five miles up the valley, set in a pinewood draw. You know who owns it?'

'I know the one but why would you want to know that?'

'I camped out in it last night, burned a mess of wood and fed my animal some hay I found in the lean-to, and wouldn't want anyone to think I stole either is all.' I noticed the woman turning suddenly, looking at me with a little more interest. 'I wondered if it would be OK for me to spend a few days there until my horse is rested.'

'And you too by the looks of it,' Mort said, smiling and pouring steaming coffee into three tin mugs. 'Sugar?'

'Please.'

'How many?'

'Three.'

'Sweet tooth, huh?'

'I ran out of sugar about three days ago, I sure do miss sweet coffee.'

'To answer your question, I have some fine but used heavy wool lined canvas jackets, and the owner of the cabin is Laura Bainbridge of the Circle B. I am pretty sure she would not begrudge you or your animal shelter, it's cold and getting colder. But you can ask her that yourself.'

The woman was walking toward me, smiling, holding out her hand, taking me in from head to toe. The scuffed spur-less boots, the open fronted thin jacket, the worn leather vest, faded Levis, her gaze lingering over the Colt I wore high on my hip. I took her hand, it was warm, calloused, a working woman's hands. She was around fifty, I guessed, maybe a little younger; grey hair can be fooling either way.

'Laura Bainbridge.'

I removed my Stetson. 'Charlie Crow, pleased to meet you, ma'am.'

'I heard what you said to Mort and of course you are welcome to the wood and the hay.'

'Thank you,' I said, for some strange reason liking her right off.

It was the grey eyes; much like the colour of her hair, they were clear, uncluttered of anything other than a genuine warmth, much as the rancher's rotund wife's eyes had been. Lonely maybe, I wondered.

It was a wild, sparsely populated country where people tended to stick together, sharing the good times as well as the hardships and for the most part welcomed strangers into their midst, knowing the present day hardships suffered by the wandering cowboys, the drifters who could not find work and not for want of trying.

'Have you come far?'

I sipped the hot sweet coffee. 'Montana.'

'Heading back to Texas?'

I must have shown my surprise.

'Your saddle rig, I saw it through the window, Texas Rigged, not that common around here.'

'I guess not.'

'On the dodge?'

'No, ma'am, I'm riding free.'

'We hear tell there has been a lot of trouble up in Montana, range wars, shootings and general mischief.'

I didn't see any point in ducking the issue. 'Yes, there has, but not trouble I wanted any part of so I rode on through.'

'Right away?'

I could not help but grin at her and she returned the smile, rather knowingly, I thought.

'I saw some of it and didn't linger. No one on my trail, no paper on me, just a desire to rest up and be on my way back to Texas where, I can tell you, is mostly a darn sight warmer than Wyoming.'

'Most anywhere is at this time of the year. You a gunfighter, a shootist, a pistolero or whatever it is they call gunmen these days?'

'I would not say that I was any of the things to which those names apply.'

'But you have been a lawman, though?' She answered my puzzled look by reaching out and touching my vest just above the heart where two pin holes made by a long ago heavy badge once hung. 'More than one badge maybe, seeing the size of the holes.'

'You are one hell of an observant lady, Miss Bainbridge, I may have worn a badge a time or two.'

She smiled again, that warm smile, and moved back, setting the shotgun against the counter. She flopped down on one of the three chairs situated around the stove, reached into the cracker barrel for a small handful of crackers, crunched on them and washed them down with coffee. 'You looking for work?'

I thought about that and said, 'Depends on what kind of work.'

'Honest work. I'll make you a proposition, Charlie Crow, if that's what your name really is. You can stay at the line shack, do it up some if you want — there are tools and lumber in the lean-to. The place is yours so long as you ride the line north to south and drive any cattle back down to the lower south pasture where there is still some grass, and to where I can reach them with feed if it gets too bad.' She thought for a long moment and I waited, nursing the hot tin mug. 'I'll pay you $15 a month and vitals, more if you have any trouble from the hill folk who think my cows are their supper on the hoof. One or two a winter is OK but sometimes they can get greedy and with you up there, they might take greater care and behave.'

'That sounds a fair enough offer.'

'Think about it, why don't you?'

'Not a bad place to spend winter,' Jennings added, 'but you will need some warmer clothes than those you are wearing. Anything you need your credit's good here if you are working for Laura. More coffee?'

I nodded. 'Mind if I smoke?' I asked her.

'No,' she said. 'Roll one for me, will you, please?'

We sat there in silence, sipping the coffee and blowing smoke in more ways than one while the storekeeper rummaged around through his racks of used and new clothing, trying to find something that would fit a six footer.

'You shorthanded?' I asked, as I tossed the end of the quirly into the stove.

'I have two hands working the Circle B, they don't like to be alone around me for some reason and so neither of them want to ride the line, it's you or nothing, not too many riders around here this time of the year. Too cold for them.'

I thought of Billy Joe Watts and the crowd we had ridden with and welcomed the prospect of a three month retreat. 'You've got yourself a line rider, Miss Bainbridge.'

She smiled, got to her feet and offered me her hand again before turning to Jennings. 'Bag some supplies he can carry. I'll send one of the boys up here in the buckboard next week, provided the weather holds off, to pick up more and bring some hay bales for the horse.' She turned back to me. 'You any good at picking out material? I need some for a new dress.' She answered her own question again with that smile. 'No, of course you are not. Loan him that new shotgun of mine, Mort, and some cartridges, double ought buck.' She turned away. 'Best take it with you, Charlie Crow, there are some big cats up there and a pistol will not stop them but a twelve gauge will do it every time. You got any leathers?'

'No, I'm riding light.'

'And there's a big cold coming.' She turned again to Jennings. 'You have anything that will fit this long-legged cowboy?'

'I believe so, that old Mex, Slim Jim Montoya, was about his height.' He reached under the counter, pulled out a scuffed pair of shotgun chaps and tossed them on to the bar. 'We buried old Jim last week, these are still warm.' He grinned at me and then at the woman and they both laughed.

Jennings walked out back and returned with a heavy canvas jacket and tossed that down beside the chaps. It looked about the right size and I noted the small round hole just above the heart and another a little lower down. I looked at the holes and then at Jennings. 'This belong to good old Jim as well?'

'No, Jim went to sleep in the saddle, fell off and got himself stomped on. That there jacket belonged to a fellow from up north somewhere, staggered in here late one evening, fell over and bled to death on the floor right about where you're standing now.'

I automatically looked down, at the dusty boards beneath my boots. Jennings glanced at the woman, I believed she was laughing again but at what I was not sure, my expression, perhaps, or maybe more likely at my gullibility. I've been hazed before, so I joined them in their laughter.

Outfitted with supplies, a new scattergun, a pair of deerskin gloves, thick woollen scarf, shotgun chaps and a thick jacket, both from dead men, I waved goodnight to the departing Laura Bainbridge and took up the offer of a night's sleep in the store's back room. After settling the big bay in one of the livery stable's empty stalls I shared a jug with Mort Jennings and we talked long and into the small hours of the morning. We talked mostly about him but also I learned a lot about the widow Laura Bainbridge.

4

The Big White

Three days after signing on as a line rider for the Circle B, I was in the yard of the shack, chopping winter logs to stack for the stove. The sun was shining its misty, winter, brassy hardest but although the expected snow had not materialized it was very cold, just maybe a degree above freezing. I heard the rattle of the buckboard minutes before I saw it, the wheels riding the hard packed frozen earth, the rattle bouncing off the stand of pines and heralding its progress. I leaned on the felling axe and awaited the cold air to chill the sweat soaked shirt on my back.

I watched while the driver, a rangy, bewhiskered elderly man, manoeuvred the vehicle around and through the trees and into the yard. The horses were steaming and his own breath was like smoke from his moustache-covered mouth, blowing out like the steam from one of those hot water springs to be found in that part of Wyoming. Roped off to the tailgate of the rig was a large sorrel horse, feisty, shaking its big head in irritation at being towed behind the buckboard. The buckboard creaked to a halt in front of the shack and the old man nodded.

'Supplies from the Circle B,' he offered by way of introduction.

'What's with the horse?'

'Miss Bainbridge reckons you need a spare, bad place to be without an animal.' He tied off the reins and looked down at me. 'Charlie Crow?'

I nodded.

'Biff Elliot. You got the coffee on? I've been on the road since sun up. The crapper frozen? I need one bad, should have gone before I left home.' He grinned. Everyone I had met so far in and around Cheyenne Wells seemed too good natured to be true.

While he was out back of the cabin doing his thing, I grained and watered the horses, rubbing some of the sweat off them with an old saddle blanket as they cooled down and I wondered about the sorrel.

'Thanks, I should've done that but I was busting.' Elliot was wheezing, his breath coming in short bursts; he was obviously a man not used to walking.

'No trouble.' I said. 'Come inside, coffee is about ready. You eaten?'

'Sure enough, Mort fed me before I set out, had trouble getting away, he is one lonesome old cuss. The town about up and dies in the winter and winter is here, just waiting to strike. If you are new to this part of the country, I promise you one morning soon you will wake up and find you have to dig your way out to the crapper.'

'The big white?'

'Bigger sometimes than you can imagine.' He finished his coffee and pulled his long fur coat around his skinny shoulders as I followed him into the yard. 'I'd best be getting back. My partner, Will Hook, he don't like to be alone with the widow lady for too long, he reckons she looks at him kinda strange sometimes, her being a woman and him being a younger man an' all. I think it's all in his imagination but you know how these youngsters think that God made them to please the ladies and not to work so hard.'

He winked knowingly and climbed back aboard the rig, picked up the traces and kicked off the brake. He waved just before he vanished in among the lodgepole pines.

For the next few weeks, I rode the line, hazing back any cattle I found in the draws and gullies, driving them down to the lower pastures where they would winter easier. It was not an unpleasant job and sometimes I rode the bay and other times the sorrel Laura Bainbridge had kindly thought to send me.

When the snow finally came, it was not as dramatic as Elliot had predicted but it was sudden and it was deep and I was not at the shack but a mile or so out, hunting a big cat that had butchered a young steer and left its tracks in the snow for me to follow, tracks that quickly vanished as a new blizzard blew in from the north and down off the Big Horn Mountains.

When the wind dropped some and the heavy snow returned, I should have made my way back right off but by then I had lost my bearings, the grey and white blending, hiding the familiar landmarks that surrounded the cabin. The freezing snow, again suddenly driven by a high wind, blew in hard from the north, not quite as hard as a southwestern norther, not a real Texas blue norther but exceptionally bad for Wyoming.

It had been over four hours since I rode out from the line shack. I had left before dark and before the fresh storm had hit, I was staggering around in the dark and afoot after putting a bullet through the head of the crippled sorrel which had fallen in the rapidly drifting snow, snapping a foreleg, cracking it like a dry stick, going down on its side and looking up at me with pain-filled, rolling eyes, almost begging for release. I holstered the smoking Colt, pulled the scarf tighter over my hat holding the brim down over my ears, and blew hard on my cold hands, the deerskin gloves offering little protection from the freezing cold. No way could I make it back to the line shack on foot even if I knew the way and no way was I going to stay out in the open, exposed to the wind as well as the snow.

It was mostly open ground where I had lost the cat's trail and I reckoned I was one, maybe one and half miles from the cabin which I thought now lay to the north of me, which meant walking against the wind should I even try to walk it. I could strike out a little to the west where I knew the ground to be rockier and where there were small stands of pine which would offer shelter and maybe a fire if I could get one going, but that would take me even further away from the shack. I thought about it for a long moment then jammed my hands into the pockets of the dead man's jacket I had bought in Cheyenne Wells, and turned west toward where the ponderosa pines grew.

I made it eventually to the nearest stand of pines but the struggle through the deep snow and the weight of the large flakes clinging to my clothes had tired me more than I had reckoned on. I was pretty well spent, done in; my legs ached, my chest hurt and my lungs were on fire from the cold air which was strange, freezing on the outside and on fire on the inside. I collapsed under the nearest tree, gathered some brush from around me and leaned my tired back against the rough bark of the nearest pine. The snow had stopped, the wind fallen away and I looked back to where my footprints had followed me into the trees. In a little while I thought, I would fish out my matches and the makings, roll a smoke, get a small fire going, wait until the morning and leg it back to the Circle B line shack. It was a plan, the only one I had. I could barely feel my feet and my hands were numb. I raked the back of my gloved hand across my face, breaking tiny icicles from my frozen moustache and waited for Billy Joe Watts or the bear.

The big bear, when it came, moved towards me and began gnawing at my leg but it did not hurt and when it had eaten its fill, the wolves took over and always there in the shifting shadows, the cold blue eyes of Billy Joe stared out at me, smiling that childlike grin at my discomfort. I figured after a while — and seeing that both of my legs were still intact — I was hallucinating. I heard somewhere that much like being exposed to desert extremes, the cold can affect a man in much the same way. Maybe it was some kind of refuge for the soul, some release from the pain endured. A reason for dying.

After what seemed a long while and

as I resolved the fact in my head that there was no bear, I thought I heard an owl hoot and remembered someone telling me one time that you only hear an owl hoot in the winter just before you die. The man who shared this supposed fact with me said a Sioux medicine man had told him that, and they knew a thing or two about dying. Then again, maybe it wasn't an owl I heard but a coyote. Yes, a shape-shifting coyote pretending to be an owl to fool me into giving up. I could not feel my nose and then began wondering if I ever had been able to feel my nose unless I touched it. A nose was just that, a nose, something stuck there on your face and you could not feel it from the inside.

I wished I had the strength to roll one last cigarette and then the bear was there again, standing above me and this time it was very real, huge. I fumbled for my handgun but my fingers were numb and the shotgun was still in the saddle scabbard on the dead sorrel. I thought, crap, what was the difference in the end, a bear, a coyote, Billy Joe Watts or old age? Dead was dead. And then Laura Bainbridge was there, kneeling beside me, rolling a cigarette and pouring whiskey down my throat, making me cough and putting the quirly between my lips and lighting it with a burning twig from the small but hot fire she had built at the base of the pine.

'You crazy old fart, what the hell are you doing out here afoot?' Laura said.

I said, 'The sorrel's dead, broke a leg. Where the hell did you come from?'

She did not answer my question even if she had heard it as my voice was but a whisper.

'You are too big for me to carry, but I have to get you back to the cabin, it's only a couple of hundred yards more, you got pretty close to it coming from wherever you have.' Her breath was warm and smoky as she bent low, her handsome hatless head popping out from the collar of a massive ankle length bearskin coat, her hair flaked with snow.

'I'll try,' I said. 'Help me up.'

Between us we got me to my feet, feet I could not feel. She wrapped my hands tightly around the tail of her pony and led the animal through the drifting snow, almost dragging me behind it and clear up to the cabin door. She led the animal right into the shack then, releasing my hands, led it back out and, I guessed into the warmth and shelter of the lean-to.

Laura was back in minutes and I was still there where she had left me, on my knees before the open fronted potbellied stove. She tossed more wood in through the open door and began stripping the frozen clothes from my body, talking, smiling, encouraging me to move, to help. She took the pan of hot water she had heated atop the stove and bathed me with a cloth and sometimes I was aware of what she was doing and at others I was still out there in the snow, waiting for Billy Joe Watts or the bear to come and finish the job, but they never came. I relaxed on to the tick mattress she had dragged over from the bunk and set in front of the stove. She wrapped me in blankets and when these did not stop the sudden bout of shivering that engulfed my body, she stripped off her clothes and rolled into the blankets beside me, soothing words and warm hands, warm, smoky breath and soft words encouraging me to come back from the cold or wherever it was I slipping away to. After a long while, the shivering ceased and my faculties began to function, an awareness of the situation suddenly engulfed me and I heard her laughter there in the sudden fire-lit warmth of the cabin.

'Umm,' she said, quietly, her face very close to mine, 'I can see, can feel you are awake, Charlie Crow.'

It was then, the moment, no other moment in time, in my life or hers would, could, this ever happen again. It was a moment I knew would stay with us for the rest of our lives, no matter what trails either of us would wander down. I looked into the grey eyes reflecting the firelight, a flash of something I had never seen before. I could feel her body, tighter and closer to mine, moving, her lips so close to mine, and heard the whispered simple words.

'You can if you would like to, Charlie Crow, and I would like you to very much.'

No more words were needed from either of us and I moved into her, made love to her there beneath the blankets and bearskin on the thick mattress and then slept in her arms, listening to her sweet breath and the whine of the wind howling once again around the line shack. I was happier in those moments than I had been for many years and the beauty of it was knowing she felt them in exactly the same way.

In the morning, the wind still howling around the cabin, I woke to the smell of frying bacon and sat up on the mattress, staring across at Laura Bainbridge as she cooked, the huge bear skin coat dragging the ground around her. I coughed and she turned.

'Good morning, Charlie Crow. Did you sleep well?' She smiled, not coyly but boldly as if to say, it was sudden, it happened, we enjoyed it, live with it.

'Like a baby,' I said, my voice a little hoarse, smiling back at her. 'What the hell were you doing up here?'

'I brought supplies, figured you would be running low and maybe we could not get up here again before the snow, but the big white came early, took me by surprise. Figured you might be in trouble when I heard the gunshot, and found the dead sorrel mostly covered with snow. It was hard to see what happened to it, and then you is all.'

'It broke a leg.'

'I know, you told me that when I found you.'

'I figured I was a long way off from the cabin, maybe a mile or so.'

'The snow turns you around, the wind changes, it is not difficult to become disorientated. Happened to many a more seasoned Wyoming man than you.'

'Lucky you came by, thought I was a goner for sure, started hallucinating . . . '

'That also happens, but it wasn't all a dream.' She smiled a wicked smile and I could not help but smile back. She was part girl and part woman, the like of both of which I had never known before.

'How do you want your eggs, Charlie Crow?'

'Over easy, boss.'

'Yes, I am your boss, you just remember that. And where did you get that tattoo?'

Forgetting for a moment that I was buck naked, I wondered what she was talking about and suddenly aware, pulled the blankets up around me. She was referring to a tattoo of a flying crow on my left shoulder. 'Hayes City, a long time ago.'

'What would you have had on that

shoulder if your name had been Parrot or Vulture?'

'I would have changed my name.'

'Any other reason for a crow?' She settled down beside me, the tin plates on our laps.

'I like them. Self-sufficient birds, bad tempered, mostly loners, they couldn't care less about us and we do not bother them so why should they bother us? Hell, I think they are rather handsome. They look black at first glance but get up close and they have a delicate pattern on their back feathers and in a certain light, they shine like gun oil on coal black water.'

It seemed like an outburst and I felt a little foolish but there was that smile again.

'My word, you do talk a great deal.' Then she shoved our empty plates clear of the mattress and crawled in beside me.

Laura Bainbridge stayed with me for four long days and nights when, sadly, from my point of view, the snow stopped and the wind changed, blowing the dry powdery flakes clear of the open spaces and leaving the road through the pines partially clear.

On one bright morning, Biff Elliot appeared with a big smile on his red face and a small, dun coloured pack horse laden with supplies in tow.

'Figured you made it before the big white hit and that you was holed up here. Not much we could do anyway, big drifts down below, no way through. As soon as the wind changed, I got up here, figuring you would need some grub.'

Laura made breakfast and coffee while I explained to Elliot about losing the sorrel and how his boss had found me and saved my life. He listened and nodded knowingly, keeping his thoughts to himself but I guess he could not help but notice how Laura Bainbridge touched my hand now and again and that we were very easy in one another's company.

I was sorry to see her go and while

the old man was saddling the horses and getting ready for the trek back down the hill, we kissed warmly, both of us I believe, sorry that the visit was over. She promised to visit again before the winter was over and maybe talk about things other than bears and dead horses. Then they were moving through the pines. She looked back once and I waved.

Laura Bainbridge was as good as her word and visited me several times over that cold winter. They were long and happy days and nights and in between her visits, I did what I was paid to do. I chased a few strays from the draws and once visited one of the small spreads of the so-called 'hill people'.

The cat killed again and I took most of the butchered carcass along with me to a rag tag family in an old soddy and a copper still in back of the trees, who were pleased with the meat and surprised to have it delivered. The old man gave me a jug and I ate steak and potatoes with them and shared their fire, staying the night. He played the harmonica and his wife and I harmonized some old songs to the delight of their four kids. I left at first light, the jug strapped firmly to my saddle.

I only saw the cat once, a big cougar, glaring at me from atop a rock, defiant, his domain and who the hell was I to trespass, to ride his road. I could have shot him, the Marlin was in my hand, the range was right but I thought what the hell, he had his place there on the mountain and I had mine. I was the intruder, the outsider and what was one dead cat more or less anyway? I wished he had known what I was thinking. I waved at him, he gave me a withering look and unhurriedly turned and vanished into the rocks. Perhaps he did know.

A week after my encounter with the cat, I was packing my gear and readying the cabin for the next inhabitant, stacking split logs and kindling, making sure the place was weather proof and better than when I moved in.

Laura Bainbridge was sitting staring into the open door of the potbellied stove at the dying fire. There was an unspoken sadness in the air. We had said our farewells on the previous night, huddled together, her firm breasts pressed against me and her warm tears on my cheeks and lips.

'Do you really have to go to Texas, Charlie?'

'It is something I have to do, it's where I started out from. I have to go back there and start out again, take a different trail, but I promise you, Laura, I will be back.'

'What is it you left there in Texas, and will you find it?'

'I think so. I was just a kid when I left, I hit the wrong road almost right off but somewhere along the line I found a better one and it led me here to you. I need to see it one more time, though, maybe I left something behind and I need to find it. I cannot explain more than that, there are no other words. There are places I have to see, graves I have to visit, a past I never really had.'

It is a difficult business explaining something to someone that you do not fully comprehend yourself. An almost impossible task really. I left when I was eighteen, I had no idea where I was going or what I would become but the trail and to where it led, forged me. I have been all over, some things remembered and many best forgotten but there are shadows that come to me, moments I should have made something of but for one reason or another did not. I could have been a lot of things but mostly I had made a living by the gun, not always using it. Sometimes my name and my reputation kept the Colt holstered, but not always. I wanted to stay with Laura Bainbridge but I knew that if I did I would always be looking back to Texas and Harry Boyd and Helen Dubois, shadows, and now there was Billy Joe Watts moving around in the darkness.

She watched me in silence trying, I

guess, to read my thoughts and failing. 'I don't really understand but I would like it if you came back to me. Can I write to you, is there a place there, an address?'

'If you really need me, write to me care of the US marshal's office in Meridian, I know the badge there from way back. If he is still there he will probably know where to find me, if not his successor will.'

'Do you love me, Charlie Crow?' She was fighting back the tears.

'Yes, boss, I do love you,' I said.

She laughed, it was all I could ask for.

5

Carol Creek, Texas

Carol Creek lay just inside the Texas border, the line defined there by the Conchos River, a tributary of the nearby Rio Grande, a growing town, once the county seat before the railroad bypassed it and ended up at Meridian, which was an unstoppable boom town, end of track and eventually the new county seat.

Lily Bouchard was thirty-two years old. A dusky, dark-haired woman, she stood a little under six feet tall. She was broad boned, attractive, with high cheekbones, soft full lips and large, dark brown eyes that had haunted and wearied many a young man in the border town of Carol Creek. Like any good-looking woman, she could be kind and she could be cruel, depending on a man's standpoint. If elderly and needy as were many of the Mexicans who lived on the old stockyard side of town, she could be an angel. If you were a young buck with love in your eyes, she would break your heart into a thousand pieces and think you the fool for dreaming. She was also the sheriff's daughter.

Robert Bouchard was not the elected county sheriff, although that was the title he worked under, but like such offices in most small towns he was an appointee, a deputy sworn in by the elected sheriff who resided in the big court house at the county seat. He was a deputy sheriff, a title only used on the very occasional visit from the circuit judge or by Sheriff Waxman himself. To such officers of the law he was Deputy Sheriff Bouchard, but to the townsfolk he was the sheriff. He was originally from Louisiana and had a hint of the Cajun about him which he had passed down to Lily, making her no soft touch for any man, certainly not in Carol

Creek, although many had tried and several, having not learned their lesson, still aspired to becoming her beau.

Lily walked into the cool evening shadows of the unlit sheriff's office where Bouchard was working at his uncluttered desk, going through fliers that had arrived in the morning's mail, his jacket tossed across the back of the only other chair in the room. Inside the office was a black, unlit potbelly stove, hat rack, gun case and notice board covered with posters of wanted men he was unlikely ever to meet this far south, but then again, you never knew. There was a solid, hard wood door between the office and the empty iron barred cells in the back of the small building. He looked, up smiled a white-toothed smile at the woman and lifted the corner of the cloth draped tray she placed before him.

'Smells good. I was intending to go down to the Green Frog for supper but this is better.'

'Sorry to keep you away, I guess you

were hoping to work some more of your elderly charm on Susan Grey. I thought this would keep you out of mischief; she can cook but I can cook better.' There was teasing laughter in her voice, a joyous sound that few ever heard. A definite Cajun inflection in her speech.

Lily Bouchard was not happy in Carol Creek. She smelled trouble in the wind and the town of Meridian was fifty miles away and the nearest ranger station over a hundred.

'Not so much of the elderly. You bring any beer?'

'I thought you had some here, I'll go get you a jug.'

'No.' He waved towards the vacant seat in front of the desk. 'I've got a jug of Dick Thomerson's homemade brew somewhere — his private stuff, not that forty-rod he sells across the bar. Sit down, let's talk. I don't see enough of you. It's late when I get in and early when I leave.'

She sat down as she was told, not something she would normally do.

'Dad,' she said, her voice serious now, 'why don't we just pull up and go back home where we belong? This place is going to come to grief and you will be right in the middle of it and I doubt anyone will lift a finger to help you.'

It was a question he often asked himself and sometimes he knew the answer and sometimes he did not but he was an older man, a man of beliefs, ideals, of loyalty. He had raised his right hand up there at the county court house at Meridian and given his word to Waxman, the State of Texas and the people of Carol County and he was a man who lived by, judged himself by, keeping his given word.

He did not answer right away, thinking about it yet again. He could quit. He had done a fair enough job of keeping order in the town, keeping the few rowdies on a tight leash, busting a head here and there when necessary. He had saved a few dollars, was liked and respected as was Lily, but there was little other than his given word to keep either of them there. It was, after all, just a job and not a well-paid one at that. Trouble was brewing but it might not come to anything, at least he hoped it would not. John H. Weldon, the new owner of the Rocking J, the largest ranch in the valley, was flexing his muscles some and pressuring the several small two-by-four ranchers and nesters in the far end of the long rich valley, but he guessed that was mainly over the lack of grass and would ease when and if the rains came and the waterholes filled and the creek flooded.

He dipped some bread into the dark beef gravy, sucked on it and chewed the crust for a long moment.

'You sure can cook, Lily.' He smiled and added gently, 'Almost as good as Susan. Maybe you ought to get a job at her place and take a few hints on how to stuff a real sweet apple pie. You are not big on apple pie.'

She laughed, knowing he was teasing her, trying to soften the atmosphere that clouded their brief moments together whenever they talked about their future or lack of it in Carol Creek.

'Weldon has taken on some new hands, not regular looking cowhands either. Three or maybe four of them are in The Longhorn, Dick asked me to mention it to you. No problem but he thinks maybe you should take a look.'

He noted the concern in her voice and that displeased him. She was the light of his life and he had no wish to worry her. He wiped his lips with the gingham napkin that had covered the meal and stood up, stretched and involuntarily broke wind.

'Pardon me,' he said, 'must have been something I ate.' He smiled again, trying to lighten the mood.

Bob Bouchard was not a tall man; his wife had been a tall lady and their daughter had inherited her size and her good looks. At that moment, looking at her and thinking back for the briefest of seconds, he was deeply saddened by a lost past.

He had dark thinning hair, a

drooping moustache as was the fashion for lawmen of the period, tobacco stained. He wore black wool pants, a plain grey shirt and black cord vest and his short barrelled Colt in a shoulder holster under his left arm. He swung a tan whipcord jacket over his thin shoulders and, reaching out with both arms, gave Lily a hug.

'Don't worry, honey. I'll take a look, probably just drifters heading for the border, nothing we have not seen a hundred times before. You take that tray back home and on the way, drop by and say hello to Susan for me. Tell her I'll maybe drop by for a nightcap after my rounds.'

He winked at her and turning the lamp down low, followed her out into the early evening, where a small breeze was flickering the lighted oil lamps that dotted the long dusty main street of Carol Creek.

Bouchard took a deep drag at the small cheroot he lit as soon as Lily left the office. He watched her walk across

65

the deserted street and into The Green Frog Café, knowing the two women would laugh together at how easy he was to tease. He liked them to think that, be that way about him, easy around the subject.

There were several horses hitched at the wooden rails along the street, mostly in front of The Longhorn. The other saloons did not come to life midweek but would be a handful come the weekend and especially on a weekend payday Saturday night. He could hear music drifting up from the Mexican part of town, a trumpet and guitar and now and again the haunting, tequila-smooth singing voice of Thomas Vargas, the Mexican town constable who kept some sort of law and order along the row of bars and whore houses that seemed to be busy any night of the week but were, fortunately, none of Bouchard's concern.

Vargas was hired by the town council and had his own way of dealing with trouble. He was a likeable man, tough but fair and he and Bouchard had a mutual liking and understanding of each other and of the other's duties within the actual confines of the township of Carol Creek. Beyond the town the county was under the jurisdiction of the sheriff's office and as the appointed deputy, his sole responsibility. As long as the town expanded to the north there would be no conflict of interest but should there be any movement to the south and the river, there might be a problem. Bouchard had no wish to see trouble where there was none and held his own counsel on that matter.

He stood still for a while, dragging on the smoke and enjoying it, liking the smell of the tobacco on the cool evening air. A man thing. He dropped the short wet stub on to the boardwalk and ground it out with his boot heel. He unbuttoned his coat and let it fall open just enough to show the hint of his piece but well clear enough to show the gold and enamel badge given to him in the Meridian court house nearly three years to the day.

Bouchard paused at the doorway of the saloon and looked over towards the swing doors, the habit of a lifetime behind one badge or another. Lily was right; apart from a handful of early evening regulars — mostly store keepers, the barber and the undertaker — there were four newcomers in the room, their faces reflected in the fly-specked mirror that ran the length of the polished pine bar. Three of the men were obviously friends chatting at the bar leaning inwards; range clothes, jacketless, each wearing a sidearm. Two of them were similar in build, the third man smaller, rat-faced, hatless, and had straggly lank hair and was in need of a shave.

Bouchard wondered what had attracted Thomerson's attention. Maybe it was the way they stood so close together or the way they spoke, but that he could only find out by going in and ordering a drink at the bar. He thought about it for a long moment and caught a closer look at the fourth man. Older than the others, pepper and salt close-cropped hair and clean shaven except for a full but not drooping moustache. High crowned Texas Stetson on the bar, the Carol County Times in front of him and a half-full glass of frothy beer in his hand. Half-closed eyes as if he found the print too small or the reading of them too difficult. A tall man in faded, much washed Levis, a high riding, tooled, black leather gun-belt, the holster housing a walnut gripped, long barrelled army Colt .45. A faded red shirt and pale blue kerchief.

Bouchard pushed the swing doors open and stepped inside. The smell of stale tobacco, and wood polish. He nodded to Curt Shultz, the German émigré who ran the thriving general store, and to Alderson, the meek little man who ran the post office and worked the telegraph when needed.

'Evening, Sheriff, buy you a drink?' Shultz, always the man with his hand in his pocket, the good friend to everyone, always ready with a kind word, a joke and a drink. The one man who really did think he had a chance with Lily Bouchard if he played his cards right and the one right way, he believed, was to be a friend of her father's.

Bouchard nodded his thanks and walked to the long bar, plenty of room there but nevertheless, the three men separated and made a space for him between them. He nodded and although they ignored him, he could tell they noted the star pinned to his vest.

'Make it a whiskey, Dick, the good stuff, and a beer chaser. First today.'

He watched closely in the mirror, the three men looked at each other and he fancied he saw a nod but was not sure. His back embraced that chill not felt in a long time. To his far left, the man reading the paper glanced in the mirror and made eye contact briefly then returned to the newspaper, licking his finger and turning the page before sipping at his beer which was flat and had lost the frothy head.

The three men were no longer engaged in any conversation; apart from the muted chatter of the two townsmen and the clack of dominoes being played at one of the tables, the room had gone quiet.

'Sorry, Dick,' Bouchard said quietly. 'I don't usually have this effect on your customers, was it something I said?'

Thomerson smiled nervously, and ran his hand over his slicked back red hair, then down his grimy apron. 'Not that I know of, Bob, maybe . . . ' He didn't finish the sentence.

'It's the badge, we don't like to drink with a badge. Cramps our style.' One of the two large men turned to face Bouchard. 'This the only saloon in town?'

Bouchard smiled; this was not what he had expected but he rode with it anyway. 'Sorry, gents, this is my watering hole and I'm not on duty at this hour, just enjoying a drink of my own time.'

'Well then, maybe you can enjoy it someplace else.' The big man's voice was low, irritable.

'Hey, what's with you men?' Shultz turned to the group.

'Butt out, Kraut.' The big man behind him joined in, his voice hard edged, cold.

'Butt out, Kraut,' the rat-faced man laughed. 'You're a poet, Jules, a goddamned poet.'

Bouchard picked up his shot glass and tossed the whiskey down. He picked up the beer, took a mouthful and set that down beside the empty glass. He had got himself into a bad place and he knew it. The belligerent man and the rat-faced man were in front of him, there was another behind him and, possibly, the fourth man reading the newspaper behind him. Shultz and the postman had moved to a table on the other side of the room. The three men were on the prod and he had no idea why. As far as he could tell he had never crossed trails with any of them in the past.

'Are you leaving, Sheriff, or am I going to kick your skinny butt across the street?'

'To be honest, my friend, I don't think either is going to happen.' Bouchard let his long jacket fall open.

The big man moved away from the bar, his hand dropping to his holstered gun. 'I won't say it again, Sheriff.'

The rat-faced man sniggered and moved clear.

Bouchard could not see the men behind him, was uncertain, hesitating. Suddenly the expression on the man's face changed and he heard a yelp and a thump behind him as the third man fell forward, hitting the boarded floor hard, a pistol bouncing off the floor and settling at Bouchard's feet.

Bouchard did not turn around; he figured in that split second for good or bad the play was made and he pulled. The short-barrelled Colt cleared the holster and was pointing right at the big man's chest, the man's hand still inches away from his gun.

'Unbuckle the gun-belts, gents.' Bouchard was fully in charge, the moment was his. Whatever had gone on behind him was at that moment of no concern. 'You too, runt.' Bouchard waved the muzzle of his Colt to take in the rat-faced man, the smile gone from his narrow face. Both men obliged, their gun-belts hitting the floor with a thud.

Bouchard stepped away from the bar, kicking the grounded handgun clear. The man behind him was splayed out on the floor, blood oozing from a wound behind his ear. The newspaper reader picked up a bar towel and wiped blood and hair from the long barrel of his Colt before slipping the gun back into the high rig. Bouchard nodded at him, the man nodded back and returned to his paper.

Bouchard said, 'You're strangers in my town and I don't want to be feeding you and seeing your ugly faces for three weeks until the circuit judge gets here, so you leave those irons with me, consider it a fine, and you take this back-shooting sack of shit off Mr Thomerson's floor and ride out. Ride hard, fast and far. I see you here again, I'll take a bullwhip to you. Ride, pronto.'

'My name's Bobby Halloran.' The big man almost spat the words. 'And that's my brother Jules your man cold-cocked, and you might have the high hand here tonight but we will be back for our guns. You can count on that, law dog.' He looked past Bouchard to where the cowboy was intent on his reading. 'And you, mister, are a dead man.'

The man turned a fresh page of his newspaper, seeming not to hear the threat or to care much about it if he had.

'Move it before I change my mind, you wouldn't want to eat jail food in this town for three weeks and that is sure enough the truth.'

He followed the three men to the doorway and watched as they mounted, the concussed man holding tight on to the saddle's pommel, grunting. He watched them clear of the town's street lights and wished he had thought to remove their saddle guns.

6

Charlie Crow

Cheyenne Wells and the Circle B were a long way to the back of the bay and I was anxious to be down by the Conchos but it was a detour I had to make, part of my pilgrimage.

Just north of the Arizona line I rode through Merritsburg, which had changed little over the long intervening years — no new builds and several of the existing ones run down and shuttered. The cemetery was rather more crowded than when I had left and it took me a while to find Harry Boyd's bleached wooden marker. I lifted my hat and stood there for a long while and for a moment, in some far off reverie, I fancied I heard him singing 'Danny Boy' in that rich baritone voice and the bawling of the cattle stilled to his gentle singing.

I had picked some Indian paintbrush on my walk up the hill and I settled them atop the small dirt mound that covered his young body, and wondered if he would be standing over my grave had one of his rounds shot and killed me instead of Jerry McCoy's green parrot, then doubted that he would. I thought about him and the shooting for long minutes and after a while I felt his shadow lighten, the burden ease and if for no other reason, the long ride back had been worthwhile. I said a quiet and final goodbye to Harry Boyd, swung up on to the bay and rode back down Main Street. Eyes were on me but I felt no desire to stop, and embraced the feeling that at least part of my journey was over.

From Merritsburg I crossed the border into Texas and headed south again. I crossed the dry lands to the north of the Rio Grande and headed a little to the east. It was familiar country and I had sworn I would never ride that way again but in a single lifetime, a man swears to many things, makes a lot of promises to himself and to others and, if he is honourable he will endeavour to keep them to those whose company he holds highly. I had promised Laura Bainbridge I would be back and that was one promise I was aiming to keep. However, promises I had made to myself, in haste, anger or, in some cases, fear, I could afford to break; after all, I was the only one likely to get hurt.

I found The Arrowhead without too much trouble. Certain landmarks had changed, trees were gone, trails grown over but water was key and the springs that fed the cold water well on the run down, two by four spread owned by Hannah Dubois, created a wide line of green right up to the old ranch building. A single storeyed house with a lean-to attached, small barn and pole corral. I sat on the bay and surveyed the place while I cocked a leg over the pommel and rolled a smoke from the Durham sack.

It was derelict and nearly blown away. The main building had lost part of its roof and the porch had caved in, leaving only Hannah's rocking chair standing on the cracked wooden boards. The pole corral was still standing and more or less intact, although some of the poles were missing and I guessed they had maybe ended up as firewood. The rope of the cold water well was coiled beside an upturned wooden bucket used only, I suspected, by wasteland wanderers on their way from and to nowhere in particular.

The barn was in better shape and I walked the bay through the open front and out the back, past the rolls of tumbleweed trapped in the dark and dusty corners of the interior. It was there where I had set it, leaning but still standing, pointing wearily to the blue sky, weathered, cracked and still bare of any lettering, the very thing I had ridden miles out of my way to see, a marker over what was once a small heap of dusty soil, the last resting place for Civil War veteran Sam Dubois. I studied it for a long while, remembering wondering why it had troubled me so over the long years and, finding no answer to that question, I turned the tired bay's head and headed west. It was at best a four day ride to Carol Creek and I was tired of trail food.

It was a town like any other I had been in, bigger than most, smaller than some. A border town. A rifle shot from Mexico. As far as I could tell, Carol Creek was split into two sections, both with a fair sprinkling of saloons, stores, billiard rooms and, certainly on the southern end which was the Mexican quarter, several whorehouses. I put the bay in the hands of the livery stable boy, telling him the animal needed a good rub down, some good feed and a lot of soft words and for this I paid him fifty cents, which was twice as much as he was expecting. I figure in this world you get what you pay for, either with dollar bills or good living. Mostly with dollar bills.

I took my trappings to the Glendale Hotel recommended by the owner of The Longhorn Saloon, which had been my first port of call and wondered if he owned them both. The Glendale Hotel sported a wash house in back and I took a double room, the only one on offer, and booked a tub of hot water in the bath house. I shucked my dirty clothes and dispatched them to the Mex laundry service as offered by the desk clerk, and soaked for an hour before putting on clean clothes and planting myself in the dining room behind a thick, well done steak. I have never been one for half-cooked meat.

I rolled a smoke and studied the street some through the open doorway. It was nearly dark, the oil lamps were lit and I chose The Longhorn for an after dinner drink, figuring in a town like Carol Creek one saloon would be much like another.

The beer was cold and I had not seen a newspaper in weeks. My backside was a little tender from the day's ride and I was happy to read an old copy of the *Meridian County Times* and stand at the bar, leaning on it, watching in the mirror and wondering what the hell was going on with the three men and the badge. Whatever it was, I wanted no part of it until the man behind the peace officer pulled his weapon and I pulled mine and cracked the barrel of my Colt across his ear.

'What the hell was that all about, Bob?' the barkeep asked, after the three men mounted and rode out, heading south. 'I never seen the likes of it. Who were those rascals and why were they on the prod after you?'

'Damned if I know,' Bouchard said.

As he leaned on the bar he was shaking. He took the refilled glass offered to him and downed it in one swallow and picking up his refilled beer, moved away and along the bar to where I was still studying the newspaper.

'I need to thank you, mister, I was in a spot there for a while.'

'You handled it OK,' I said, not looking up.

'Buy you a drink?'

'A beer would be good, this one kind of died on me.' I nodded at the flat, half glass of beer in front of me.

'Dick,' Bouchard called over his shoulder, 'a fresh one for this gent.'

The barkeep pulled a glass and slid the frothy beer along the counter. The lawman stopped it and handed it to me with his left hand and holding out his right hand at the same time. 'Bob Bouchard, and you are?'

I don't know why but I hesitated a moment and then took the offered hand. 'Crow, Charlie Crow.'

'Thank you, Mr Crow, you did me one hell of a favour there.'

'It was nothing, I don't like back shooters is all.'

'What do people call you, Charlie? Chas? Chuck?'

'Crow is good but mostly they call me Old Timer.' It was a line I liked to use.

He laughed. 'You and me both, though you have got to go some way yet to catch up with me, I'm guessing.'

Suddenly there was a swish of a dress, fresh cotton, gentle perfume as a tall, good-looking woman swept into the room.

'Dad, what the hell went on in here? Curt says you were almost killed.'

'Language, girl, we have a guest.' He nodded in my direction. 'Meet Charlie Crow.'

She seemed to notice me for the first time, studied me some then offered her hand. It was a firm handshake, almost manly. 'Lily Bouchard, pleased to meet you, I'm sure. Please forgive my outburst.'

Bouchard said, 'Mr Crow here just did me a big favour, honey.'

'What happened?'

'Please excuse me,' I said quietly, for some reason wanting to be out of there and clear of their company. 'It's been a long day, a long ride and I need some shuteye.' I nodded, then feeling a little foolish, picked up the newspaper I had been reading, put on my hat and, touching the brim in the woman's direction, I left them there.

* * *

Carol Creek offered two reasonable eating houses as recommended by the hotel desk clerk, The Green Frog Café or the Rosebud. His preference, however, was for The Green Frog, I suspect on account of the handsome woman who ran it.

'What can I get for you, Mr Crow?' she asked, after I had settled on a table facing the wide doorway, open early in the morning and letting in a fresh cool breeze which would be smothered when the sun rose high and the heat dropped down, wrapping itself around the town like a hot towel. She could see I was surprised she knew my name and she added, 'The whole town knows of you now. We value our sheriff highly; he may be a bit long in the tooth for the job but he keeps the peace fairly and would never take a kick back, not even a free breakfast.'

Old in the tooth, I thought, trying to remember where I had recently heard that saying.

'Name's Charlie,' I said.

'Susan.'

She offered her hand. I stood up, took it, held it for a moment longer than necessary. It was a cool hand, matching her demeanour. She was a mature woman, had hazel eyes and dark red hair speckled here and there with grey, and not an unattractive lined face. Crow's feet, laughter lines maybe. I guess she had been around some but she coloured nevertheless and I released her hand saying, 'Three eggs over easy and some ham, a coffee and some toast if that's OK.'

'OK, Charlie, three eggs it is.' She smiled and I wondered why she didn't ask me what I was called (the usual response) but she accepted my given name.

The eggs were good, not swimming in grease as is so often the case, the ham was tender and the coffee a rich, dark, aromatic Joe. I sat back and pulled the recent paper I had swiped from the hotel lobby and flicked through the pages, noting that the big dry was everywhere and beginning to cause some concern to cattlemen all over South Texas.

First her shadow drifted across the printed pages and then I smelled her, the same fresh aroma from the night before with maybe just a touch of jasmine. I looked up, pushed my chair back and started to my feet but she hushed me and, pulling the chair opposite me from under the table, asked me if I minded her sitting down. Then she waved to Susan and asked for a coffee without waiting for my reply.

'I hope you don't mind me joining you, Mr Crow, but I have something I need to ask you.'

'Charlie,' I said, 'please call me Charlie or just plain Crow if you prefer but the mister makes me feel even older than I am. A young man called me sir yesterday, I nearly pistol whipped him.'

I smiled so she could tell I was not being serious.

'That's your forte, pistol whipping? I hear that's how you saved my dad.'

'I find it a lot quieter and certainly less messier than shooting a man, even a back shooter.'

'Dad says it is the trademark of a good lawman. He thinks he has heard of you. Has he? Are you a man of the law, Charlie Crow?'

I shook my head.

'Have you ever been?'

I ignored the question, offered no answer. 'That what you came here to ask me?'

'No, no, it isn't. Actually I came here to warn you.'

'Warn me?'

'About what you bought into last night when you floored the Rocking J hand.'

Susan said hello, smiled and placed a

coffee in front of Lily Bouchard.

'A refill, Charlie?'

I could see the use of my name caused a momentary flicker in the younger woman's dark eyes. I nodded.

'Be a moment, fresh brew boiling.' And she turned away.

'I didn't buy into anything, ma'am. The man was out of line and I put him back where he belonged. Nothing more than that.'

'I doubt that is how John Weldon will see it, he does not like his men taken so lightly, especially by a stranger. He believes it shows a lack of respect.'

'And that is his problem, not mine. How old is this John Weldon?'

'Your age, I guess, late forties or early fifties.'

She had me pegged right there. 'You think I am that old?'

'Maybe it is just your hair and moustache. One longer and the other shorter would take a few years off you.' She smiled and I smiled back. 'Why do you ask?'

'I knew a John Weldon one time, my first riding job as a kid but that was West Texas and he would be about ninety now if he lived this long.'

'Weldon is from West Texas, sold up when his father died a few years back and bought the Rocking J for a song. Could be his son, I guess. What was he like, his father?'

'A fair man, an honest rancher, he had a son who would be about my age now. The man was blond, tall, maybe taller than me.'

'Sounds like a ringer. But our John Weldon is not a fair man. John Carol, one of the founder members of this county, owned the Rocking J and ran the valley fair, figuring there was enough water and grass for all. Come round up, all the cattle were bunched and sorted and he took care to see that any unbranded stock were shared. This man wants the whole valley for himself. He fenced off a couple of water holes and part of the upper valley, cutting off access to some of the creek. When the

91

creek looked to be running dry he fenced off more. It has caused a lot of bad feeling and some violence. He has also imported a few gunmen, three of the newcomers you met last night, and Dad is in the middle of it.'

'Bad place to be.'

'Yes, it is but he won't quit, says if it gets real bad he will contact the Rangers or maybe the US Marshal in Meridian.'

'I wish him luck with that but I am only passing through and am no threat to your Mr Weldon. I will be gone before he knows I was ever here, but thanks for your concern.'

'How long did you work for his father?'

Susan brought the coffees and I waited her departure, thinking a long time back. 'About a year, I quit right after I buried Hannah Dubois's old man.'

'Her husband?'

'It's a long story and not a pretty one.'

'It's been a long time since anyone told me a story and I do have all morning and Susan's coffee will keep me awake should I doze.'

I liked Lily Bouchard right from the off and I like to talk so I told her the story just the way it was, just the way it happened.

'Hannah Dubois was the wife of an old Civil War veteran, Sam Dubois, they moved out west from Louisiana, he only had one leg and half an arm — '

'How did he have half an arm?'

'I don't know, fact was he only had half an arm and he was probably the shortest man I ever saw. They had two fat, lazy sons that looked like they may have eaten a third child had there ever been one, and they ran about a hundred or so head of scrub cattle which gave them the right to pack them on to the Weldon drive, even though they were in poor condition on account of the lack of grazing around their no account outfit which consisted mostly of rock, rattlesnakes, gila monsters, sand and scrub. The John Weldon I worked for was that kind of a man.'

Lily Bouchard settled back in her chair and sipped the steaming coffee.

'Hannah Dubois was a skinny, wrinkly, mean-faced little woman with a look that could cut a man in half so he could never be put back together again. I only ever saw her smile that one time all the while I was there, that one smile early one dark morning when we were branding and her old man had found himself some corn whiskey and stumbled around the fire on his peg leg. He was waving the jug in the air, but he tripped on a root and fell, the red hot iron he was carrying along with jug, jammed forward and stuck their Arrowhead brand on to the backside of the laziest of the two kids. He screamed a blue norther, the old man swore, the cow bellowed and she smiled. Just that one time, she smiled and her smile lit up the world like nothing I ever did see.'

'You ever see her again?'

'That next spring Weldon sent me up there to collect whatever they had and bring them back for the drive. I wasn't hankering for that chore but by then I was on the payroll as a full time cowhand, so I saddled up and rode out to that dust hole of an Arrowhead. She was there sitting on the porch in a rocker, just like the first time I saw her, face like doom, thinner than I remembered even. He was hopping around and seemed pleased some to see me. We set out there and then, cleaned out the coolies in two days and brought down twenty-four head of crow bait and branded them in the corral with me, keeping him well away from the branding iron.

'All afternoon I could feel her looking at me but she was grim-faced, sitting there and never saying a word to either of us. I ate a cold silent supper with Mr Dubois, said goodnight and bedded down in the barn, although they had offered me one of the bunks vacated by the sons when the pair of them up and hightailed it to California in search of good times and gold. They sure were backward, them two boys, the rush was long gone.'

'Maybe they just needed to get away,' Lily said thoughtfully.

'Maybe. Anyway, around four in the morning, she poked me awake with the handle of a pitchfork and says she needs some help up at the cabin. Seems old Mr Dubois got himself a skin full of moonshine that night after supper, tripped over his peg leg and fell down the cold water well. I pull on my pants and go take a look-see. Sure enough, I can see him down there in the water, clinging on to the bucket with his one arm wrapped around it and his hand on the rope. He does not weigh much on account that he is small and only has the one half arm and one leg so I wound him up and hauled him over the side and girl, is he stiff, deader than Dan's donkey.

'She just looked down at him then up at me and asks me to bury him — just like that, flat out — in the soft ground back of the barn and offers me a dollar for doing it. Well, I'm young and that's a full day's wages to me so I agree, got me a shovel and dug a hole. She is still standing over the old man and has laid out a small tarp for his shroud. Trouble was he had such a grip on the bucket line I couldn't get his hand free.

'While I'm thinking what is the best thing to do, she goes into the cabin and comes out with a ball peen hammer and smashes his fingers real hard several times, then peels away the rest of the broken hand and looks at me as if to ask why I didn't think of doing that. I get the tarp around him and drag him over to the hole and I roll him in. I tell her I think he landed face down and should I get in the hole and roll him over? She tells me no, that's the direction he was headed anyway.

'And this is where it began again. Like a warm morning summer sunrise, first a glow on a distant horizon and then, slowly, the rim of the sun appears and that glow spreading slowly across the land but, in her case, it was the beginning of that same smile and the warmth spreading upwards through her skinny cheeks and up to her pale blue eyes. A smile to die for. Feeling a little awkward, I asked her if she wants to say a few words over her old man and she just keeps on smiling, shakes her head, turns and walks back to her rocker on the cabin's porch.

'Well, I filled in the hole, found a short board of old lumber in the barn and stuck it end up over the grave as a marker, figuring when she was over the shock of his passing, she would write his name or something on it at a later time. I put my hat back on, gathered up my gear, saddled the pony and got ready to mosey the cattle back to where the drive was gathering. She is still sitting there smiling but the smile has changed some, no longer a smile really. Oh, the shape was right but it no longer reached her eyes and seemed set on her face like a ghastly mask. Where there had been brightness and light was only darkness. I can tell you I felt real bad about taking her dollar but I did and shook my head at the offer of breakfast, thinking the sooner there was a lot of country between me and Arrowhead, Hannah Dubois and the late Mr Dubois, the happier I would be.

'I told her I could write on the marker for her or she could do it later, but she just fixes me with that awful grimace and tells me she and God knows who he was and that is all that matters. Cold, just like that and still the face never changing, not even as she spoke. I got her to sign the release to sell her cattle in Abilene and gave her the receipt the boss had given me to give her once I filled in the details. She did what I asked and then just stared at me, that damned smile fixed on her face like some kind of death mask like the ones you see in the travelling shows that come to town in the summertime. Like I said, the shape was right for a smile but it just wasn't a smile anymore. It was a kind of a nasty, empty thing. I told John Weldon about what had happened when I got back to the herd and he just nodded and said not to worry, she was a crazy woman anyway.'

'You ever see her again?' Lily asked.

'No, I quit the drive in Abilene and headed on out to Arizona, never intended to go back there, not ever. For years I could not get that picture of her out of my head. I dropped by there on my way here, though, somehow I could not resist it. I figured she would likely still be sitting there in that rocker with that smiling mask fixed on her dead face, thinking about old Mr Dubois face down in the ground with no name on his marker and just the thought of it sure enough gave me the shivers.'

'And was she still there, sitting, smiling?'

'No, it looked for the most part as if the Arrowhead had simply dried up and blown away, but I am glad I made the detour. I think she will be gone from my dreams now, at least I hope she has.'

'You tell a good story, Charlie Crow, but is it true?'

'All of it. Well, mostly, give or take a word here and there.' I smiled and she smiled a good one right back at me.

We finished our coffee and she shook my hand once more and left. I got to my feet and watched her walk out into the sunlight, a tall, straight woman and I wondered why she was still unmarried.

* * *

I wasn't too sure I wanted to hang around in Carol Creek. On the one hand I had a few dollars saved and just so long as I was careful, I could spin it out for a month or two and rest up and be certain there was no law on my back trail. Range wars tend to create bad feelings that linger long after the gunfire has faded. I had kept a pretty low profile in Wyoming and only Billy Joe Watts had known which way I was heading and in any case, it was a county war and the responsibility of an elected sheriff and it was unlikely I'd have attracted too much attention from the federal law officers. Also, I found Lily Bouchard an attractive woman and I had a bucket load of stories I could tell.

On the downside, if I stayed around, I would inevitably get sucked into their impending war and if that were the case, I would have to be on the side most likely to win and that, as usual, would be where the most muscle was and that was not with the small ranchers but with John Weldon. Also, it had nothing to do with my ride back to Texas. It was a problem but I had a couple of days to think it over, see what happened and then move on if I so decided and I was curious about John Weldon.

But it seems time moved swiftly in Carol Creek.

Outside in the street, the air was thick with the smell of rain on the gentle breeze drifting down from the high hills that surrounded the valley and the air was dark, foreboding almost. I walked across the rutted dusty street to the hotel and asked the wizened little desk clerk for my key, adding that it looked like rain. He said it was like that every morning but it never came, it went on down to Juarez and gave the Mexicans a good soaking. He handed me the key on its chunky wooden tab, saying there was a gent in the billiard room wanting to see me.

'Did he ask for me by name?'

'No, sir, he asked me your name, the name of the man who coldcocked the Rocking J hand. I told him, I hope that was OK. He would have checked the register anyway had I not told him. He's from the Rocking J, the top hand I believe.'

I nodded. 'That's OK, most people around here seem to know my name by now.'

I left him there looking a little perplexed and made my way across the lobby to the small, dimly lit games room. My visitor was not a big man; slim, dark-haired, late thirties, I guessed, in a well-washed blue denim shirt and jeans, a grey Stetson riding low on his head. He was not wearing a sidearm. He looked up as I entered, smiled a big, white-toothed smile, walked to meet me, holding out his right hand. I took it, a big hand for such a narrow man, a firm handshake.

'Jim Keen, ramrod out at the Rocking J. Good to meet you, Mr Crow.'

I did not feel warm enough toward him to tell him the name was Charlie so I just nodded and waited.

'Hope you don't mind me coming here like this, sir, but John Weldon asked me to call in and invite you out to the Rocking J for supper this evening. He sets a fine table.'

'Why?'

'Sir?'

'Why would John H. invite a complete stranger to dinner?'

'I have no idea, I just carried the invite is all. Maybe he heard something about you or maybe he just wants some new company. If you don't wish to ride out there, I will give him that message.' There was no threat there in the statement, yet I felt the smile and the benign invite were not things to be ignored.

'How far is it?'

'Four miles, maybe half an hour away. Just take the southern road out of town — you can't miss it, the main gate is signposted.'

'Tell Mr Weldon that I will be there around six o'clock, and thank him.'

He gave me the big winning smile again, nodded and left. He simply seemed to glide out of the room, lithe and probably very quick on his feet, and I thought maybe Jimmy Keen didn't need a six-gun to impose himself upon others, those big hands would make big fists.

* * *

I decided to rent a buggy, my backside was still a little sore from the pounding it had gotten on the long ride from faraway Wyoming. The livery stable owner checked that there was oil in the lantern in case I returned after dark and that there was a blanket under the seat, were it to be a cold evening and told me he would add the cost of the rental to my livery bill and wished me a pleasant evening.

Thirty minutes was about right and I turned off from the sun-baked trail on to a wider roadway leading to a large gate over which, suspended from a lodgepole pine cross railing, was a large iron Rocking J brand. Simply the capital letter J at an angle riding a half moon. There was a mounted guard at the gate, packing both a sidearm and lever action Henry rifle.

'Whoa, there mister, you have business here?' He moved his pony alongside the buggy, looking down at me. I do not like to be looked down upon.

'Mr Weldon is expecting me and I am late, don't piss him off by making me later than I already am.'

'You Charlie Crow, the guy who coldcocked Bobby Halloran's little brother?'

'Are we going to discuss my life story or are you going to let me through? If it is the former be prepared for a long evening, if the latter get your pony out of my face and that gate open, pronto.'

'OK, keep your shirt on, I was just checking is all. If I was to let anyone through here not expected it'd be my butt; I don't win either way.'

He turned his mount back toward the gate, leaned down and raised the iron fixing and the big gate swung open under its own weight. I pushed the buggy on past him and tipped my hat to him.

It was only a short ride from the main gate to the wide, open fronted ranch house. Cottonwoods surrounded the back and sides, and the front of the stone house was dominated by a large, circular cold water well beyond which was a long hitching rail, the uprights interspersed with summer flowers, the perfume from which drifted across to me, stirred by the gentlest of an evening breeze. There was a tall lodgepole pine flagpole from which drooped a lone star Texas flag.

Although not dark, the rocking moon was clearly visible in the early evening sky. I reined in the pulling horse and before I could climb down, Jimmy Keen stepped down from the porch and took the animal's head, leading it forward to the rail. He smiled that white-toothed smile at me, nodded and stepped back on to the raised porch and disappeared into the shadows.

'Happy that you were able to come, always delighted to have a visitor for supper.' The voice gentle, almost soothing, a you-can-trust-me sort of tone. A voice to be wary of, probably sounded the same when either happy or angry with you. He was a big man; hatless, wearing a tan suit, florid sunburned face, dark eyes contrasting with a flow of long blond hair and

Buffalo Bill goatee. I guessed his appearance, his grooming was calculated and quite deliberate; you dress like the best and folk might really think that you actually are the best.

I climbed down from the rig and he reached out a hand to me.

'John Weldon, sir, and you are Charlie Crow, it is good to meet you. Your reputation precedes you, sir.'

I took the offered hand; it was a firm handshake, not a hard grip, more of a gesture to impress his manhood upon you yet still strong enough to require that you trust him. John H. was all image and the double of his old man.

'Come inside, Mr Crow, you are forgivably a little late and I am a hungry man.'

I followed him in through the heavy double doors, across a polished pinewood floor to where a dining table was set for three. Although a warm evening, there was a fire burning in the wide open fireplace; for effect, I supposed, more than for any practical purpose. Leather and polished furniture, a walnut gun case and a smattering of paintings depicting various heroic actions of the US Cavalry, several trophy deer heads. It was a man's décor; the only oddity was a vase of red roses on the dining table.

'My wife will join us shortly.' Then turning to the Mexican woman who offered to take my jacket and hat, he said quietly, 'Maria, tell Mrs Weldon our guest has arrived and we will be dining in five minutes.'

He turned back to me, the smile again. 'A pre-dinner drink, I think, Mr Crow, a nice Californian red. I brought in five cases this morning.'

I nodded. 'Thank you and the name is Charlie or just plain Crow, the mister makes me feel old.'

'Of course, Charlie it is, although some of those townsfolk who feel close to you in Carol Creek refer to you as Chuck.' The smile broadened to the old I'm-your-friend smile which obviously was as practised as the handshake.

'Please call me John.'

He went to the dining table, poured two glasses of decanted red wine and carried them over to where I was standing, staring up at the large portrait of a tall rider astride a large white saddle horse. The man was gazing straight down at me from the painting, his puzzled eyes boring into me like he knew me but could not place me. I don't like being looked down upon and that was twice in an evening.

'I do not have any people close to me in Carol, I only arrived in town yesterday.'

I wafted the glass under my nose, sniffing the contents and swirled the red liquid around the glass. The wine was a dark red and tasted like it smelled, of wild fruit. I smiled my appreciation.

'You like it?'

'I like it,' I said. 'I like it very much.'

'You know something, Charlie, I have several businesses in Carol and I was in town this morning early and before nine o'clock, I must have heard your name a dozen times over. The stranger who saved our sheriff and pistol whipped a Rocking J hand. They appeared to enjoy telling me that, you have any idea why, Charlie?'

'Not the faintest idea. All I did was stop a drunk yahoo from becoming a drunk killer.'

'Sort of thing you have done before, I don't doubt?'

I did not answer but sipped some more wine, it was good.

'Heard so much about you I thought it would be nice to meet you, you sounded sort of out of the ordinary, not too many men would buy into a deal like that. You sounded like a man I might be able to use.'

'Use? I don't ever get used, John.'

'A figure of speech, I meant no offence.'

'None taken.'

'You seem taken with the portrait, it isn't me, you know.'

'I know,' I said, 'it's your daddy, Big John. I rode for him when I was a kid.

The Slash W, a West Texas brand.'

'You rode for my old man?'

There was genuine surprise in his voice, an irritation that he had learned something he could not possibly have known had I not told him. Something that was connected to him, his past.

'I never met you. I didn't get invited up the big house and you did not frequent the bunk house and, besides, you were back east most of the time. Schooling, we were told.' Then I added just for the hell of it, 'I'm the waddy who buried Hannah Dubois's old man.'

'I'll be damned. That story went around for years, I never knew if it was true or a made up campfire yarn.' He suddenly burst out laughing. 'I'll be damned, the man who buried old Sam Dubois.'

'Not a dirty story, I hope.' The woman moved across the pine floor, her dress swishing. She was smiling a genuine smile. 'A glass of wine, a fire any time of the year and a story or two is a man's paradise. Is it shareable?'

Weldon turned, a look of irritation quickly vanishing. 'My wife, Josie. Josie, this is the man I was telling you about, the stranger in town who saved our sheriff and floored one of our new hands.'

'Charlie Crow, ma'am.' I held out my hand; she took it, gave it a gentle grip.

'Please call me Josie, ma'am makes me feel so old.'

'A feeling we share,' I said.

'You get called ma'am a lot?' She laughed.

Josie was a small, handsome woman, with short cropped black hair streaked with grey, a small mouth offering a petal shaped smile and dark, no nonsense eyes. I guessed she was my age.

'Well,' she said, 'is it suitable for a lady to hear?'

Before I could answer Weldon said, 'You remember the Hannah Dubois story back at the Slash W, well, this is the cowboy who hauled her old man out of the well and buried him face down, old Sam Dubois, the peg-legged Civil War vet.'

'What a strange coincidence,' she said, the smile widening, looking at her husband, asking him with her eyes a question I could not read.

'Yes, it is, isn't it just?' he said, his quizzical look matching hers.

The food was good and although my steak was a little underdone for my taste, it was sweet and tender and no great chore to eat. The wine flowed although Weldon did offer me beer or just about any other liqueur available, while he himself switched to tequila halfway through dessert, when we enjoyed a plate of apple pie covered in fresh cream. Conversation was sparse, neither of them offering much of themselves. The weather, cattle prices, the lack of respect believed shown to Texas by the federal government, rustling and what he referred to as the Carol County's squatter problem came up instead.

After dinner, Josie excused herself,

saying she would join us later for coffee but right then she had chores to attend to. I could not begin to guess what those chores were left for her to do in a house seemingly alive with servants including the ever present Maria, who followed her from the room like a puppy dog.

Weldon picked up his drink and took a store bought cigarette from a polished wooden box on a side table, offering me one. I shook my head, preferring to roll my own and we moved out from the warm room and on to the cooling, covered veranda.

'The Lone Star State,' he said softly, waving a hand at the dark, star-studded sky above us. 'She's not alone tonight, there must be a million of them up there.' He paused. 'Which one do you think is ours, Charlie?'

'Any one of them will do, I guess.'

'Not sure the Mexicans or the settlers or the two by four scrub ranchers in the valley would agree with you there, they all seem to have their own idea of what

Texas should be.'

'Well, maybe they have that right just as you and I do.'

'Right, Charlie?'

I rolled a second smoke, thinking of where this was going and not liking the direction too much. 'The fundamental right of all men being considered equal as defined in the constitution. Little men can dream big dreams as well as big men can dream little dreams.'

He smiled at me almost benignly, I thought. 'I guess your daddy fought for the Federals in the War?' It was a question.

'A hell of a lot gone between the War and now,' I said.

'You are a curious man, Charlie Crow, a cut above the drifters we see around a border town like Carol Creek. You have a voice. Where were your people from?'

'It does not matter where my folks come from but if you are really that curious, we moved from back East to West Texas when I was just a kid, and my old man and my mother both worked themselves to death running a two by four scrub ranch like a lot of folk in this valley. Finally they quit when the big ranchers thought they needed to be bigger than they were. Something I have never understood about some people, they always want more than they actually need.'

'My,' he said quietly, 'I seemed to have touched a raw nerve. I am sorry, again not intentional.'

'Not a problem,' I said. 'Your daddy took me on, gave me a start, a start I appreciated, made the most of.'

The conversation kind of died out after that and when Josie did not reappear due, according to Maria, to a sudden and bad headache, I took coffee and brandy after which I said goodnight, thanked him for the meal, shook his hand and climbed back aboard the buggy which had been delivered to the doorway by Jimmy Keen.

Weldon followed me down the steps and looked up at me. 'You did not wear a handgun this evening, is that usual?'

'I did not intend to shoot anyone tonight and that is not usual either.'

We both laughed but I believed we laughed for very different reasons.

7

Jesus O'Brian

I spent the next couple of days exercising the bay, the tenderness having left my butt and the restrictions offered by the buggy making a tour of the valley useless. I rode the draws, noted the open waterholes and those the Rocking J had fenced off. As long as there was water in the creek, which in turn was fed by the Conchos tributary which itself was reliant on the Rio Grande running high, things were not too bad. Big trouble was the Rio Bravo, the name given to the border river by the Mexicans, was not running high and the Conchos was already low, so low in fact that the shallow parts of Carol Creek were already showing bottom.

I stopped by one of the small outfits

for water and was welcomed by the owner Jesus O'Brian. Half Irish and half Mexican, he was a dark-skinned, middle-aged man with a wide smile and a ready handshake. He invited me to a small noon meal of freshly baked bread, butter, cheese and onions all prepared or grown by his wife Gloria, a Texas lady with a brood of small children at her skirts, their wide eyes staring at me. A boy, the eldest, who was around ten years old, fixed his eyes on my Colt before going out and petting the bay and feeding him pony nuts.

'Been here ten years, just beginning to get ahead and the Lord blesses me with a drought and John Weldon both in the same summer. Fucked if I know what I ever did to deserve this.'

O'Brian and I were sitting on the stoop, our backs leaning on the uprights out of earshot of his wife or the kids, smoking rolled cigarettes and drinking strong black coffee laced with something he called potcheen, a white spirit of some kind that had one hell of a kick to it.

'Better than that forty-rod they sell in The Longhorn. Got me a small still back in the hills, share it with my neighbours, malted barley or sometimes potatoes, even sugar beet, one hell of a leg shaker if you drink too much of it. The US Marshal, Wally Dade, drifts by now and then but turns a blinder, packs a jug in his saddle bag when he leaves.' O'Brian laughed. 'I guess Weldon drinks that wine piss he gets from California and ships to Carol, maybe a glass or two of this would drive away some of the darkness that seems to drape around him like a shroud.'

'He ever threaten you, harm you?'

'No, he hasn't, leastways not directly. Fenced off Dillon's Wells, a seep to the east of here. Some of his men ride by after dark now and then, let off a few rounds to scare the kids. Found a dead milk cow up the valley, turned out it wasn't mine but a stray from George Buck's place, got his hundred and forty government acres a little ways up the valley, but it could have been mine. He tried to buy me out but I wouldn't sell, couldn't sell, where the hell would I go? I put ten years of hard work and I do mean hard work, back breaking work into Shamrock, even a big handful of dollar bills could not buy me those years back. The wife agrees so we keep a loaded shotgun by the door and I have an old Smith I can shoot if necessary.' O'Brian's voice suddenly took on a more serious timbre and he stared off into space, sipping his coffee. 'But I do not want it to come to that, I really do not, no winners down that road.'

He offered to show me around but I told him I was heading back to Carol Creek, wanted to be back there before dark. As we shook hands he said quite suddenly, 'You the drifter who pulled on a Rocking J hand the other day, cold cocked him?' My surprise must have shown. He smiled. 'Word travels fast around here.'

I did not answer and I do not believe he expected me to anyway. I climbed aboard the bay, tipped my hat to his wife and gave two bits to the kid for looking after my horse.

'Be seeing you,' I said.

'Any time, mister, always a welcome at Shamrock.'

I was back in Carol Creek just after dark. I left the bay with the stable boy at the livery and flipped the boy a quarter to care for the animal.

'Has he got a name, mister?' he asked me.

I told him no but he could give him one if he so chose, but nothing fancy. He seemed pleased and led the tired horse into the darkness of the stable, whistling a really out of key Dixie.

It had been a long ride and I was dusty and hungry. A meal or a bath? I opted for the food and made my way along the darkened street towards The Green Frog.

The place was empty, perhaps too early for diners or maybe that's the way it always was in Carol on a weekday night. I had no way of knowing but Susan seemed pleased to see me and while I was waiting for my well done steak, several suited townsfolk wandered in; a couple nodded to me but most paid me no attention and that was the way I liked it. Soon after my steak was devoured and my coffee served, and I was into the two day old newspaper that had been left by the noon stage driver, Sheriff Robert Bouchard came through the doorway. He looked around, saw me and headed my way.

'Mind if I join you? I hate eating alone.'

I indicated the empty chair with a nod of my head. He sat down with a sigh and ordered a rare steak from the attentive Susan. She seemed pleased to see him too and I guessed there was something between them, and I wondered if his daughter knew about it.

I read the newspaper and he chewed on his steak, which was seeping blood and I wondered if it was really dead. After a short while, he pushed the plate to one side and set about the apple pie and cream he had ordered with it.

'For a man with a big appetite, you sure keep pretty trim,' I observed casually but he chose to ignore the observation and even the note of envy I had injected into the remark.

'You had a busy day, Crow?' he asked. 'I have been pushing paper and that for some strange reason gives me more of an appetite than if I had been chopping cotton all day.'

'You ever chopped cotton, Sheriff?'

'A figure of speech, and please call me Bob, most people do. No, I've never chopped cotton, never really done anything physical, been behind a badge one way or another most of my life. Started out way back when it seemed the right thing to do, when the country was growing and needed law, and now?' He shrugged. 'Now I don't know. It isn't the job it once was, no black, no white, just a dirty grey and you have to lean one way or the other to see which colour it ought to be.'

'Why do it then?'

'You've been behind a badge, Crow, that I can tell. You may be a drifter now, a fiddle foot, but I have you pegged for being a lawman at one time or another. Am I right?'

There was no point in denying it. 'I have done most things in my life, wearing a badge was one of them.'

'Old time? You ever meet any of the real lawmen?'

'Such as?'

'Masterson, Wes Harper, Luke Short, Wally Dade, Earp, anyone like that.'

'I bumped into Dade one time.' I smiled, thinking back to the wash and the man on the paint horse. 'Spirited old man, but it was only briefly. Wyatt, yes, I rode with Wyatt Earp.'

'The hell you did!' His eyes fired up, he leaned forward, 'What was he like, I mean really like?'

'What was Wyatt Earp really like?' It was a good question. Sitting in The

Green Frog café thinking back to younger days and my encounter with the famous lawman, the moments flashed by but it was too long a story to tell even if I had the inclination to do so . . .

I had been on the train carrying the Earps when it arrived in Tucson after his brother Morgan got bushwhacked. I was just a young man who should never have left the cowboy life but I had a taste for cards and was tired of the smell of horse sweat and cow shit. I saw Wyatt going after Stillwell and Ike Clanton, the pair had been laying for him with the idea of doing him mortal harm. I was only a railway guard back then and carried a shotgun. When Earp looked at me, we made eye contact and Earp remembered me from somewhere back in the day, probably when I was briefly dealing faro in Wichita and he was the town badge. He nodded to me and I nodded back and leaned on the car door, indicating I would watch over the crippled Virgil and the family while he ran down Stillwell and Clanton.

Later, as everyone knows, he did run Stillwell down and blasted him, with a shotgun and pistol. Clanton, as usual, made a run for it and got lost in the night. Earp thanked me and told me if I ever needed any help the Earps could give me to just holler.

Next time I met him, I was sitting on a corral fence out back of a run down two by four ranch in Arizona Territory, owned by an outlaw and Clanton associate named Indian Charlie Cruz. There were about thirty scrawny cattle in there behind me and three ponies.

One sunny morning, Wyatt Earp rides out of the dust and rests his horse in the yard. The only other person present being a vacant-eyed, tow-headed kid peeling spuds and dumping them into a tin bucket. Earp nods to me just as Cruz steps out of the crapper. He takes a couple of steps towards Earp and stops dead, recognizing the big man. Indian Charlie wears his gun rig low, a cross draw rig on his left hip which is unusual seeing as he was a lefty. His trick was, though, while an adversary was watching for a show of movement from his right hand, he would pull his short barrelled Colt with a sweep of his left, turning it as he drew and he was quick. Wyatt Earp never really gave him that chance, though.

Wyatt says to Cruz, 'I'm on the hunt for Ike Clanton, Charlie, you seen him?'

Cruz says, 'I've never heard of the man.'

'Never heard of Ike Clanton?' says Earp in mock astonishment.

'Never, and who the hell are you anyway to be riding in here and asking questions of me?'

Earp sighs. 'Is this going to be one of those dumb conversations, Charlie, where I ask sensible questions and you tell me stupid downright lies, one of those kinds of conversations?'

'You calling me out, Earp?'

Earp nods that he was doing just that and without further ado, pulls his piece and shoots Indian Charlie Cruz twice in the chest. The man goes backwards into the corral fence, slumps down and stares up at Earp in bewilderment, saying, 'You shot me.'

Earp looks over at him and says quietly, 'It sure looks that way,' and then to me, 'You in on this, son?'

'No, sir,' I say, 'I just work here is all.'

'And the boy?' Earp nods to where the boy is still peeling spuds, seemingly unaware of the demise of his employer.

'He just works here, same as me.'

Over by the corral, Indian Charlie is struggling to get to his feet. Blood is foaming from his mouth, and he's muttering, cursing. Earp looks over at him, cocks the piece and shoots him in the head just above where his nose met his eyebrows.

'Doing what exactly?' Earp asks me.

'Brush hunting those mavericks in the corral, bringing them down here. Charlie pays us, well, he used to pay us fifty cents a head so we got maybe ten bucks coming to us.'

He looks over at the kid.

'Thirty beeves, you got fifteen dollars coming to you, split it fair with the kid. Have you seen Clanton?'

'No, didn't even know this was his place or we wouldn't have signed up.'

'They Mex cattle you brought in?'

'I don't know, they don't talk a lot as I've heard.'

'You funning me?'

'No, sir,' I say, 'not at all, them animals is surely dumb. If they are Mexican, it's news to me.'

Earp smiles, climbs down off that big sorrel of his and looks down at the dead outlaw. 'See what money he has on him, take what's yours and get his trappings together — you may be able to sell them somewhere down the line. I'll keep the Colt and gun-belt, and if he has a carbine, you keep that. Turn the cattle loose but bring the horses along, no point hanging out around here. Clanton sure as hell won't be back this way.'

'We going somewhere, Mr Earp? You arresting us?'

'No, but I don't want you out here. I'm riding under a Deputy U.S Marshal's warrant and I got tired men, trigger happy deputies combing these hills for Clanton, Curley Bill Brocious and the rest of those damned back shooting assassins, and I don't want you to fall under a federal bullet, you'll be safer riding with me. If you want to ride on with us when we get clear, that's OK with me. You want to go on to wherever you want to go, then that is also OK. Up to you, now get it done and bury that piece of shit while you are at it.'

* * *

That's how it went down but it was a story I really did not want to tell so I gave Bouchard the outline, the bare bones and left the rest to his imagination, knowing that he would embellish it somewhere, someplace when retelling it on some distant warm evening to friends over cigars and a jug.

'He took a shine to me, I guess, and we were good friends after that, and I rode with Wyatt on and off for a while till he got it done or gave up. No one is sure about which way that went but there sure were a lot of bodies spread around that part of Arizona and no one was sure how they met their ends.'

'Lily said you tell a good yarn, Charlie Crow, damned if you don't.' Bouchard said, smiling.

That evening, upon an invite from Bouchard, I joined him for an after dinner sundowner. I was surprised at the invitation but secretly delighted if it meant spending some more time with Lily Bouchard. I asked him if she would mind my turning up and he told me it was her idea, something about being a storyteller. He had winked at that and I sensed that maybe there was some sort of conspiracy going on between them but to be honest, I didn't really care. I was just passing through and would soon be headed back for Wyoming and Laura Bainbridge but I had just as well enjoy myself in Carol Creek as not.

We had barely settled down to our coffee and brandy when there was a loud banging on the door and Bouchard beat his daughter to it. He opened it, incautiously I thought, to reveal a red-faced and wheezing Dick Thomerson. The Longhorn owner was short of breath and took a moment when guided into the house by Lily.

'What the hell gives?' Bouchard said, quietly, calmly, handing the man his untouched drink.

'That Rocking J puncher, the kid Crow pistol whipped, Jules Halloran, he's in the Longhorn and on the prod calling Charlie here out. Says he going to shoot his eyes out among other things . . . ' His voice tailed off as he threw back the whiskey, then he added with an attempt at a wry smile, 'Glad I gave you the good stuff.'

Bouchard gave a weary sigh and refilled the glass, handing it back and saying, 'Is he drunk, Dick?'

'No, sir, stone cold sober.'

'Is he alone, no brother with him or that ratty little guy?'

'Not as far as I could see and the street's pretty much deserted, being midweek and all.'

'OK, you sit tight, take it easy. I'll deal with it.'

'Dad, don't.'

Lily Bouchard's voice had a pleading edge to it, she looked desperately in my direction. I got to my feet and walked over to the hook from which Bouchard was retrieving a gun-belt and swinging it around his skinny waist. I put my hand gently on the older man's shoulder.

'My fight, I think, Sheriff, let me take care of it.'

Bouchard looked at me long and hard in that quiet room, seeing something maybe that I did not. He shook his head.

'My town, my job. I will not have citizens taking the law into their own hands, that's the way of the vigilante. You've worn a badge, and you know that. This man is my responsibility, it's what I get paid for.'

He smiled and buckled the belt, then carefully tested the Colt, lifting it and dropping it back into the holster, making sure there were no snags.

'Maybe so but I started it and I need to finish it. Besides, he might not be alone.'

'Dad, please listen to Charlie. You do the job because people around here know you, respect you. This gunman does not. He will kill you.'

'Lily is right,' I said quietly. 'He may just cripple you but for sure he will not give you an edge.'

I could see the man thinking on it, weighing something up in his mind. 'You are right about one thing, Crow, he might not be alone. There is a way, but you will not like it.'

'And that is?' I said.

He turned his back on me and walked over to the leather-topped desk and opened a small side drawer, reaching in and then turning back to me, holding out his hand. I looked down at the silver star stamped out of a shield with the word 'deputy' at the top and 'sheriff' at the base.

'Pin that on and you can deal yourself in. If not, shut up and do as I tell you. And don't look so surprised, I know you have worn one of these or similar in the past.'

The room went very quiet, only the wheezing of Dick Thomerson broke the silence that followed.

I looked at Bouchard long and hard. I had told myself I would never get behind a badge again, wearing it over your heart, a target. Who the hell would be fool enough to do that, knowing that? Me, I guess.

I took the badge and pinned it on to my vest, at the same time reaching for the makings, shaking the dusty tobacco from the sack and on to the brown rolling paper, an act, a pierrot's performance, a clown. I pulled the tab tight with my teeth and fired the quirly, blowing the smoke into the air.

'You want me to raise my hand, swear my loyalty to the Lone Star State and Carol County or can we just get it done and get the hell back here for a drink?'

I winked at the startled Lily Bouchard, who had taken all of this in without once interrupting. Not like her, I figured, and that, for some strange reason, pleased me.

'Sorry, but I have to.'

I raised my right arm but he just laughed, waved it down and said, 'The hell with it, I guess you know what to do anyway.' He crossed the room again and opened a closet door, going in and coming out with a sawed off Greener in one hand and a box of shells in the other. 'I'll back you, watch the street just in case Dick here is wrong.' Then he added, 'Dick, you go back to the Longhorn, keep an eye out but nothing foolish. It's not your job, it's the badge's job.'

'Be careful, please, both of you.' Lily barely whispered the words.

Bouchard nodded then turned to me. 'This could be the start of it, you know that, don't you? Whatever happens in The Longhorn could be the first real shot fired. Weldon is waiting for a reason, for someone to die, that's how range wars begin, one shot at a time.'

I took my gun-belt from the back of the chair where I had looped it as soon as I had entered the house, buckled it on and slapped my hat on my head, tipping it forward just a fraction. 'That or just a gunny on the prod. Either way, it has to be dealt with and I will try to disarm him if possible.'

'I know you will.'

Then we left the house, not looking back, me loosening my gun in its holster and the old man shaking shotgun shells against his ear to be sure there was lead in them before clunking them into the open choked double barrels of the shotgun.

'Like back in the day,' he said, and I smiled to myself, just momentarily thinking it was, then feeling the weight of the star and not liking it.

I looked through the fly speckled window straight into the smoke-filled bar of The Longhorn. Thomerson was nervously polishing glasses with one eye on the job at hand and the other on the batwing swing doors. The storekeeper Shultz was sitting at a corner table facing the bar; he and four other light-suited dignitaries including the hotel clerk were shuffling a worn pack of Bicycle playing cards, seemingly unaware of the danger they might be in if a gunfight ensued and lead began to fly. There was a smattering of drinkers at the long bar where Jules Halloran was standing, his gaze fixed on the doorway reflected in the large mirror. He was not drinking, simply staring and rolling a cheroot around his wet lips. He was jacketless and his holstered gun tied low down on his thigh. That was something else that always puzzled me, why wear it so low? In the first place it was uncomfortable and in the second, it made no difference to the speed of the draw.

I looked across the street and saw Bouchard move across a lighted alleyway before ducking into a doorway directly opposite the saloon. He waved and I waved back, took one last drag at the quirly I had fired when we left the house, dogged it, stuffed two wads of cotton in my ears and stepped through the swing doors and into the saloon.

It was like some kind of magic show, a puppet master waving a wand, pulling strings. As soon as I entered the room, the bar cleared as men moved to the left and the right, like the parting of the Red Sea I had seen a picture of in an old family Bible. The card players quickly moved to the side of the room, their game forgotten and Thomerson dived down behind the bar, only Halloran did not move. He glared at me via the mirror, smiled and spat out the cheap cigar he had been sucking.

'So you finally found the sand to call on me, you old piece of shit.'

He did not turn around and his voice

was without anger, very matter of fact which in itself was a little worrying. An angry man in a gunfight is usually less of a danger than one who is calm, almost reflective. I hadn't really thought it through but I remembered disarming a kid in similar circumstances and wondered if it would work here this night. It was worth a try.

'Didn't want to disappoint you, kid, needed to finish my dinner is all, you know how it is.'

'No, no, I don't know how it is, suppose you tell me just how it is, Old Timer.'

I stepped clear of the doorway but stayed where he could see me. 'I don't like to kill a man ever and certainly almost never on an empty stomach.'

'I see the badge, it makes a fine target.'

'I know, that's why I am wearing it, give you something to shoot at.'

'Your fat mouth will do.'

'Colourful. But before you go for that gun, I just hope you covered the barrel with axle grease.'

There it was, just the hint of hesitation in his movement, then the full turn to face me. 'And why would I want to do that?'

'Because when I take that gun away from you, it will ease the pain when I ram it up your backside.'

I have never experienced such a quiet, such a mantle of nothing that fell across the room. When I had tried this line in a long forgotten town called Primrose in Wyoming, again behind a badge, the kid, along with the rest of the customers, had burst out laughing and was still laughing when I relieved him of his firearm and marched him off to the lockup.

But Jules Halloran was not laughing, he was suddenly angry and as his hand dropped to his Colt I knew I had lost him. I wanted to say don't do it, to scream the words but it would not have made any difference to the outcome and even as he drew, I pulled and shot him twice through the heart. One round stayed in him and the other cracked the mirror behind him, losing much of its velocity as it passed through his body. He rocked back from the impact of the slugs, regained his balance and stared at me although I knew he was not seeing me, only the darkness that was enveloping him. The gun dropped from his hand and he went down on his knees then, bent at the waist, and leaned forward, staying there as if he were praying to the fallen weapon.

Even as I watched him, wondering, what if he had been a little faster, did I leave it too long, try too hard to take him alive, I heard the roar of the Greener out in the street behind me and a shriek of pain. I turned to the door, Colt cocked, but it was Bouchard who came through the swing doors, the sawed off shotgun in his hands, black powder smoke drifting from the barrels of the weapon to add to the stink and the white cloud wreathing the room from my own weapon. He smiled at me, a mirthless smile.

'You were right, the ratty runt was in the hotel doorway, and is still there. You OK?'

I nodded. 'I've been better.'

I opened the loading gate of the Colt and shucked the two spent cartridges, amused as Thomerson emerged from behind the bar and picked them up, looking at me for approval. I nodded. He was shaking scared but not so much as to miss the opportunity, knowing the brass would be a talking point sometime and maybe worth a dollar or two.

⋆ ⋆ ⋆

Long before Old Doc Owens opened up his hotel and the billiard hall in Carol Creek, the latter with the added attraction of ladies upstairs, Owens had been a fair country doctor who quit his practice to go hunting gold in California. He was years too late and he did not find any gold worth a damn, but he did find that his knowledge as a practitioner of medicine put him in high demand in a vast country where doctors were still few and far between, and those that were in practice were usually horse doctors who tended humans on the side which was OK if you had bloating or hoof rot.

Jack J. Owens's reputation was greatly admired and folk with any kind of an ailment travelled far and wide to be treated by the good doctor, and his services were paid for with the goods of their particular trade if paper money or silver coin were not available. Cattle were common, milk cows or beef, sheep, produce of all kinds and when none of the former was available, well, then there was gold dust. And with the gold dust tucked away in a San Fernando bank, Owens upped stakes and settled in Carol County in the Lone Star State of Texas, telling his Californian friends, with a smile, that there was 'gold in them thar pills' and he was taking his share back to the state of his birth.

Owens put up his shingle, Jack J. Owens MD, opened up The Glendale Hotel and bought out the local livery stable, one of the general stores and opened his own bank. He was a kindly, fair man, popular with the locals and a good friend to Robert Bouchard and his daughter. And it was part in spirit of friendship and part out of his natural duty as a physician that the dark suited, grey-haired old man was in Bouchard's kitchen, sipping whiskey and giving the elderly counterpart what he considered to be sound advice.

'You have to face it, Bob, you are not a young man anymore. Sure you are pretty fit for your age but had that drifter not been there the other night and taken the badge this night, we could well be measuring you up for one of Ike Jezzard's pine boxes.'

'You saying I should quit, give up the badge, ride out with my tail between my legs, Doc?' Bouchard said, a bitter edge in his deep voice.

'I'm just saying what I'm saying is all.'

'What exactly are you saying, Doc?'

'Did he keep the badge or hand it back?'

'You know damned well he handed it back. Gave it to me with that damned silly smile as soon as the smoke had cleared.'

'So you are on your own again and this valley is about to explode and now, maybe, a damned sight faster because of this shooting. Weldon will take that as a sign of you taking sides and he will not be a happy man about that.'

'I'm not taking sides, I'm just upholding the law. It's what I am paid to do, you know that.'

'What I know is the fact that you are not being paid enough.'

'I'll not quit, not in my nature.' He waved his empty glass toward the bottle at Owens's elbow.

The old doctor topped up the glass with the amber liquid. 'This will not help.'

'Maybe not but it won't hurt either.'

'You are one stubborn man, Bob, best thing you can do if you want to stay behind that badge is to get this drifter, this Charlie Crow, to take back the star. Is there any chance of him doing that?'

'Damned if I know.'

'Best you find out sooner rather than later then.'

8

John Weldon

I walked into the welcome cool shade of the hotel lobby and asked the desk clerk for my key. As he handed it to me he looked over my shoulder, and I saw something in his tired watery, eyes that looked like they had seen it all before. I turned to see the Rocking J ramrod walking towards me and this time he was wearing a gun. He smiled.

'Mr Weldon would like to see you, he is in room twelve and he asked would you like to join him for supper. He will be eating in his room.'

'I already have plans for this evening.'

'Would you care to tell him that yourself, please? He's a kind of shoot-the-messenger man.'

He smiled and shrugged like it would be fine if I did and not too worrisome if

I did not. There was something about the man I liked.

'Sure, I'll tell him myself, wouldn't want to get you shot.'

Weldon opened the door, beamed that warm smile at me and held out his hand. 'Come on in, Charlie, and thank you for coming.' He turned to Keen. 'Jimmy, get Charlie a drink. Whiskey OK?'

I nodded, watched as the foreman topped up a glass and dropped in some ice from a bucket by the small dining table which was set for two.

'You will join me for supper, Charlie?'

'No, thank you,' I said, noting the disappointment in his expression, 'I have a dinner date tonight.'

'Lily Bouchard?' He smiled. I did not answer. 'Pity but maybe another time perhaps. You have time to finish your drink and maybe converse for a while?' Again I said nothing but sipped the spirit, it was good, smooth, darkly amber.

The Rocking J owner poured another for himself and turned back to me. Keen moved across the room behind me to my right.

'I don't like people standing behind me,' I said quietly.

The big man waved his hand and the light-footed Keen moved toward the door and I heard it close behind him.

Weldon indicated a chair and I took it, happy to get off my feet for a moment or two. I had been walking that afternoon, pumping through the sagebrush with a scatter-gun I had borrowed from Bouchard's office and bagged a fat, wild turkey for supper. Wild turkey prefer to run than fly but this bird took off, bursting out through the sage and I dropped it with the choked barrel at around fifty yards.

I take no great delight in killing animals but recognize that someone has to kill your meat. The area was rich in game and I fancied that when the big dry was over, the creek would run with fish. A realization hit me at that moment out on the prairie that it would be a right nice place to settle down and the wrong place for a war waged by a man who wanted to buy the whole valley with gunfire.

Upon delivery of the bird and the return of the long gun, I had been invited for supper which was what I was auguring for anyway. I wanted to be in Lily Bouchard's company; it was as simple and as clear as that, and required no deep thought as to the reason of it. Looking across at Weldon, I wondered if it would be worth my mentioning that fact but decided against it as being the wrong time and the wrong place.

'Jules Halloran's brother wanted to come in and take you down this evening but I talked him out of it for now, but he will probably try sometime without my sanctioning it, so be on your guard.'

'I always am,' I said, 'but thanks anyway. I have been expecting him, but not face on like his kid brother. He will try from an alleyway or from behind a rock someplace.'

'Are you not interested in why I talked him down?'

'Because you like me?'

'No, because, Charlie, thanks to the telegraph, I know a lot more about you.'

I did not say anything but reached in my vest pocket and took out the makings carefully, rolling a quirly and waiting for Weldon to continue.

'You would have killed him same as you did his brother. You see, Charlie, I know you rode with Wyatt Earp and Wes Harper. I am reliably informed that you have worn a badge in several counties and even a deputy US marshal's shield on two occasions. I also know you were involved in the Johnson County fracas. You are a walking, talking, hired running gun and men who know you walk around you.'

'You could have asked me outright, I would have told you, saved you some time.' I blew out some smoke and watched it hang there before it slowly dissipated.

'You wore a badge the other night but I don't see one on your vest right now. Did you quit?'

'It was a part time job only.' I smiled, but he did not return the smile, staring at me, thinking, weighing me up, wondering how far he could go.

'There is trouble coming to the valley, rain or no rain. To be candid with you, I want the whole valley wet or dry. Of course, I could hire a dozen guns but I like to go for the best first and they tell me you are one of the very best.'

We both listened to the silence, broken only occasionally by the chinking of the ice as we drained our glasses.

'And what of Bouchard? He's sworn to uphold the law you want to break.'

'I think I can handle the sheriff, don't you?'

I stood up and stretched, moving over to the curtained window and looking out on to the hot, dusty and deserted Main Street. A dog wandered out of the alleyway opposite the hotel and raised its leg upright against the boardwalk, turned and sniffed at the effort and satisfied, continued his journey up Main Street, once dodging a flying hoof as he passed too close to the rear end of a rail hitched pony.

'The telegraph is a wonderful thing, Mr Weldon, but it is a two way street so to speak and I've also learned a lot about you.'

'And?' There was irritation in his voice.

'I had a great respect for your daddy, he was a big man in every sense of the word. A fair man, he respected the small local ranchers, gave them a fair shake, an even roll of the dice and they in their turn respected him. There was no trouble even when water was low or the price of beef dropped; they faced it together.'

'And where did that get him? He died broke, busted flat is where it got him. I had to sell the ranch and what cattle we had at thirty cents on the dollar, it got me just enough to buy the Rocking J.'

'You could have stayed and worked it through, a lot of folk did.'

'I could have, yes. I could have run those two by four outfits into the ground and maybe taken that valley but it would have brought me trouble, local trouble I might not have handled there but here, here is different, here is wide open, just the valley and a county seat fifty miles away. I can take it without interference from anyone, not the sheriff and even the federal law stands little stead this close to the Mexican border.'

'That's your plan? You really think it will be that easy?'

'Ride with me, Crow. Ride against me and you will be a dead man.'

'No more mister nice guy then. No more Charlie, Chuck or Mr Crow?'

'Make light of the offer if you will, but keep out of my way.' The change in him was sudden and abrupt, almost childlike, like we were playing happily and I had suddenly swiped his spinning top.

I tossed back the last of the Scotch and set the glass on the table upside down, then turning, I left the room, nodding to Jimmy Keen sitting on an upright chair close to the door. I felt I had made a bad enemy but I had no choice, and wondered if I should saddle and ride clear or if the deputy job was still open.

* * *

Josie Weldon was studying a large, hand drawn map spread out on the desk top, a scaled down picture of the area surrounding the township of Carol Creek. She was dressed in Levi jeans and a plaid shirt, and a cheroot dangled from her thin lips. She had coloured sections of the map with children's crayons purchased from Shultz's store. Some sections of the map were circled and straight lines drawn across other areas. The map ran from where the Rio Grande and the Conchos met and on to where the Carol Creek picked up the feed from the Conchos. Here she had drawn large circles at each meeting place.

Weldon walked into the room, looked briefly at the map then moved to the side table and poured himself a large whiskey from a half empty bottle.

'A little early in the day for that, isn't it?' she asked.

The big man ignored the remark and moved to her side. 'Quite the little strategist, aren't we.' It wasn't a question.

Josie said, her voice angry, 'Did you meet with Crow?'

Weldon was red-faced, his body, full of whiskey and anger. He carefully refilled his glass and stared at her. He was used to the tone, the riding he knew would come but he answered her in kind.

'Yes, I did, he gave nothing away, turned his glass upside down and left me standing there.'

'What does that mean, turning the glass upside down?'

'I am not sure but I think it was either an insult or some kind of challenge. He's a wiley bastard, I think he has got himself a hankering for the Bouchard woman.'

'Good luck with that, bitch isn't interested in men as far as I hear. Not our problem though, is it?'

'The man is one hell of a problem if he sides with the law or the trash in the valley.'

'You cannot let that happen, we cannot let that happen.'

'I've sent for more men and one in particular. We will have to wait and see is all.'

'Why not turn Halloran loose?'

'Yes.' The big man stared into his glass. 'Yes, why not. The man is aching for it but not face on like his brother. Crow is too fast that way.'

'There are other ways, John.'

'Yes,' he agreed, the beginnings of a

smile touching his thin lips. 'There most certainly are.' Then changing the subject, he added, 'What are the circles for?'

'Simple, we fence off the waterholes, and we dam the Conchos and, cutting off its feed to Carol Creek, the creek will run dry almost immediately. The dirt in the valley will react and the men you hired will take them out but it needs to be done swiftly. Not like Johnson County or Lincoln County. Before there can be any federal reaction it will be over and the two-bit ranchers will either be dead or on the move.'

'And Bouchard? What of the sheriff and maybe Crow if he buys in?'

'Do I have to think of everything around here, for heaven's sake? You have men coming, make sure they can do the job, and no border riff raff like Johnson County.'

'Why are you so sure the rangers or even US marshals will not interfere?'

'Too complicated this close to the border. Blame it on the Mexicans in any event; you do it right, it will all be over in a couple of days, water under the bridge.'

John Weldon sipped his whiskey and studied his wife; she was a driven woman and a driver of men. He was not her first husband; the man had accidently shot himself while out hunting deer, or so the story went. Weldon had not wanted to sell up in West Texas but she had convinced him that he needed to grow, and that a war down there would create such a furore that the feds or the state would interfere, while in a backwater like Carol County, it would hardly make the newspapers. It was a strategy that would likely work or at least succeed enough to be too late to do much about should the law want to take a hand.

9

Wild Turkey

Wild turkey can be tough, tougher than old saddle leather, but Lily Bouchard was a fine cook. She skinned the big bird, jointed it, pan fried the joints along with bacon rashers in a black iron skillet and then casseroled it, along with vegetables in the big kitchen stove. It was a peaceful evening and although we did not know it, one of the last such evenings to enjoy in Carol Creek.

After supper I offered to do the dishes and was glad my offer was turned down; I can be a mite clumsy around crockery. Lily shooed the two of us out on to the porch so that we could smoke and take a shot or two, telling us she would join us for coffee later.

I settled on the double swing seat, wondering if Lily would join me there;

it would be nice to be close to her. A warm feeling was suddenly dashed when I thought of the difference in our ages; she was around thirty years old and I was just about old enough to be her father. Then I thought of my promise to Laura Bainbridge who was waiting for me in Cheyenne Wells, and I felt a little ashamed of myself.

'Something troubling you?' Bouchard offered me a refill from his bottle.

'No, sir, just thinking is all, and enjoying the peace and quiet. It's been a long while since I ate such a fine supper and settled myself on a porch swing.'

'You are not the greatest liar in the wilderness, although you do spin a good yarn. Lily told me about Hannah Dubois and you working for John Weldon's old man, and I told her the one you spun me about Wyatt Earp.' He laughed and I laughed along with him, it was that sort of evening.

Lily eventually joined us and Bouchard made some excuse and said he needed an early night. We talked for a while about nothing, me on the double swing seat and her on the rocker vacated by her father — not quite what I had planned but I supposed it was for the best.

'Time I was going, Lily, thanks for the supper.' I got to my feet and stood there staring out into the darkness while she went back into the house for my hat. I settled it on my head and made for the steps but she reached out and touched my arm, held me back. When I turned she was smiling.

'Do you fancy a ride out tomorrow to O'Brian's place? I have some things for the children and Gloria, they are old friends.'

'I would like that,' I said, and quickly left should she see my delight.

'Shall we say ten o'clock at the livery then?' she called after me.

I waved my yes and kept walking.

★ ★ ★

Lily Bouchard was already at the livery stable when I arrived freshly shaved, walking in through the slight early morning haze created within its dark interior by the warmth of the horses. I loved the smell of a freshly cleaned stable, the animals, the leather saddles soaped for the morning riders, and the sound of a horse snorting, breaking wind or crunching on pony nuts or fresh hay. It was a good morning and I was looking forward very much to sharing it with the young woman.

'Ready for a ride, Charlie? You happy with a strange horse?'

'What's wrong with my bay?' I asked, the concern apparent in my voice.

'No worry but Luke says Trigger needs a new shoe and the smithy hasn't turned up yet this morning.'

'Luke? Trigger?' I asked. 'Who the heck are Luke and Trigger?'

She laughed. 'Luke is the stable boy you told could name your horse. He likes Trigger, says it sounds like a big name for a big horse.'

'Is that OK with you, mister?' The boy Luke emerged from the shadows leading the bay, dwarfed by the big animal.

'Sure it is, son,' I said, smiling at the boy and winking my eye at the woman. 'Sounds like a fine name and I doubt that anyone else will ever own a horse with such a name. But you be careful around him, Luke, he seems friendly enough but he can turn mean and bite your butt if you show your back to him.'

It was the kid's turn to smile. 'He already tried that, sir, but we come to an arrangement. He don't bite my butt, I don't bite his.' Still chuckling, he led the bay back to a stall and reappeared with a large sorrel. 'This'un will suit you, name's Ben.'

'Ben is a fine name too.'

I flipped him a quarter, gave Lily a leg up, creaked myself into the saddle and we rode out into the bright early morning sunshine, heading for the hill country and the O'Brian ranch. It seemed like it was going to be a great day but I guess the fates that rule us, that guide us through our days, had other ideas for Lily Bouchard, me and a horse named Ben.

We did not take the longer direct wagon trail to the Shamrock but the quicker way up through and over the rocky outcrop that stood between it and Carol Creek. The narrow trail up through the rocky gorge was hot, the air was settling on the hot rocks and there was nowhere for it to go in the breezeless morning so it just hung around. Once clear of the rocks we would be in open range, find the trail more well-defined and, hopefully, the air a little cooler. Lily Bouchard led the way and I was happy to follow in her dust rather than her in mine, it was the gentlemanly thing to do and I was out to impress, to what real end I knew not but that is how it was. It may have been what saved her life.

The 30.30 bullet when it came struck my horse in the neck. The animal staggered and blood spouted from the hole; the round must have wrecked the main artery and as he keeled over, I smashed my leg against a sharp outcrop. I somehow managed to get clear of the saddle as it snorted in pain and fear. I grabbed my Marlin from its scabbard and slapped the rump of Lily's horse hard with the barrel, yelling at her to get the hell out of there and not to come back. At the same time, I flattened myself behind the dying horse as two more rounds cracked down, both absorbed by the animal's straining belly. Lily hade made a run for it and I rolled towards the hidden shooter, over to where the overhang would give me some protection. The man was high up, and shooting downhill even for a good shot is not easy.

I paused to catch my breath and to check the Marlin, jacking a shell into the breech and lowering the hammer to half cock, the only safety on the weapon. Some shale drifted down from above and dusted my hat but other than that, there was silence from above although the echo of the shots still resounded in my ears. I took off my bandana and wrapped it tightly around my cut leg, just above the wound. It hurt but was not life threatening.

Bent almost double, I inched around the rock face, pausing every now and then to listen. Once I thought I heard some scrabbling above me and waited but no shots rained down. About a hundred yards along, I found a cleft in the rocks leading upwards, narrow but climbable. I removed the spurs I strapped on when faced with an unfamiliar mount and laid them on the ground where I could find them later, should I survive the bushwhacker's attack.

I rested frequently then, removing my high crowned hat, putting the carbine on to full cock and taking a deep breath, I peered over the rim.

It was Bobby Halloran. Squatting on one knee and trying hard to look over the rim himself. I wondered why he had not moved and then I could see his problem; he had little room within which to manoeuvre. He had picked a bad spot for a bushwhacker, his only exit being the way I had come up and he had no visual of me, no way of knowing where I was should he climb down.

I straightened. 'Drop the gun, Bobby, or I will shoot you where you stand and enjoy doing it.'

Halloran froze, then turned, his hate-filled eyes piercing mine. Seeing the blood on my Levis, he smiled and tossed down the rifle, slowly turned his back on me then spun around again fast, a big Colt in his fist. I shot him three times, working the lever of the Marlin as fast as the action of the weapon would allow me. Each round was a killshot, no question about that, straight through the heart. He fell backwards and outwards, his arms reaching for the sky, the pistol still tightly held and his grey duster billowing around him like he was flying. I heard him hit the rocks below and when I reached the edge and looked over, I could see his twisted body stretched across the belly of the dead horse the stable boy had called Ben. I felt no pity for Halloran but some for the horse and was only glad I had not ridden the bay.

I climbed back down, wearily, slowly, and at the bottom I reset the crude bandage. Almost within minutes, Lily Bouchard was back at my side. She told me that she had been hiding across the dry creek bed and had seen Halloran's stately fall from the cliff top, had seen him spread-eagled against the blue sky, grey duster flapping like wings, falling like a shot bird.

Together we stripped the saddle and trappings from the dead horse and stowed them where they could be found. We could do nothing with Ben; nature would take its own course and in a few days, the buzzards would have done their work and only the bones would remain and then they too would eventually be dispersed by the coyotes or cougars that ruled such high places.

I located Halloran's Rocking J branded dun pony and we once again set out for O'Brian's spread. I promised myself I would personally return the animal to Weldon and tell him where he could find his late employee's body but I doubted he would give a second thought to bringing it home.

O'Brian's wife and Lily Bouchard fussed over my leg and I quite liked it, sitting there in the small dining room sipping his potcheen while they washed the leg wound which, although still weeping a little blood, was mostly scrape and bruising. The three jagged cuts could be stitched by Doc Owens and the bloodied Levis cut up the seam to get at the wound, and then Lily could repair them when we got back to Carol Creek.

★　★　★

I bought new snug-fitting, black wool pants from Shultz's general store and a three quarter length, dark whipcord jacket and vest to match and, after taking a long soak in the hotel's bathhouse, I changed into my new clothes, dispatching my blood-stained and dusty range clothes to the Mexican laundry. The Levis had gone to Lily for repair; I would have hated to lose them since they had been with me a long time. I looked at my reflection in the bedroom's cracked mirror and felt, once again, every inch the lawman. The new badge was pinned, as usual, just over my heart. A very temporary appointment as a favour from Bob Bouchard for one job that needed doing by me and only me.

I polished the black, tooled, leather shell belt and the holster purpose made for it by a fine Mexican saddle maker in Laredo, the holster being made and shaped to fit snugly but not tightly, around the large frame of my Army Colt .45 with the yellow ivory grips and the six inch barrel. One of the grips had a hairline crack and some of the dark blueing had worn from the cylinder and the end of the barrel, otherwise it was a fine looking weapon and one that had served me well and one which, with any luck, would serve me well as a deputy sheriff newly sworn to uphold the law in Carol County for just one day.

The gun had a history for me.

I wore my rig higher than most, figuring that shooting straight is more important than being the fastest on the draw. All too often I had seen men who were quick but could not shoot worth a damn. That's how I got the Colt.

Earl 'the deuce' Smith was a wannabe gunfighter and outlaw working in and around Hayes City where I was, very briefly, behind a deputy US marshal's badge helping out the local peace officer, Harry Boudine. Smith wandered into the long bar of the Cattleman's Saloon one evening where I was enjoying a quiet drink and hoping to get into the big Saturday night poker game there. Earl was surprised to see me standing by the bar and thought I was there for him. I wasn't, but he called me out anyway and as he was a known outlaw and a wanted man in the state of Kansas and I was sworn to take him in, I had no choice in the matter even if it meant ruining my poker game. Before I could say anything, though, he braced me, called me a few dirty names and told me to pull. The customers in the bar fled like rabbits when a coyote approaches or an eagle darkens the sky above them. They jumped well away from the centre of the bar room, leaving a clear wide avenue between Earl and me. He pulled fast, very fast, beat me in fact, but in his haste he discharged his weapon just as it cleared leather and shot himself in the left foot and while he was hopping around and screaming blue murder, all I had to do was clip him with the barrel of my pistol and get a couple of cowhands to take him over to the doc and then on to jail. I picked up his gun, the one I wear now, and recognizing it as being a fine piece, I kept it seeing as he was not going to need it for around fifteen years, the time the circuit judge gave him for felonious assault, cattle rustling and bank robbery. Earl 'the deuce' Smith was no great mastermind of a criminal but he had been an industrious one.

I made my way from the hotel to the livery stable at a gentle pace. My leg hurt more, I think, from the stitching job Doc Owens had done on it than from the wound itself; he would have made one hell of a poor milliner. Jeb, the livery man, was not around but Luke was there in the gloom, sitting on a bale of hay whittling on a piece of kindling and from the look of the pile of chippings around his feet, he had been at it for a long while. I sat down beside him and he shifted over a little but did not look at me.

'You want I should saddle Trigger for you, Mr Crow?' His voice was moist, tear laden.

'No, son, I want you to get the buggy ready for me and saddle and tie off the Rocking J horse I rode in on last night.

Will you do that for me?' He nodded and started to get to his feet but I reached out and pulled him back down beside me. 'I am so sorry about Ben, he was a fine horse, probably saved my life taking the bullet that was meant for me.'

'Did he suffer any?' I could smell the tears.

'No, son, it was a clean killshot from a high powered rifle, he did not feel a thing.'

'You sure of that, Mr Crow?'

'I was on his back, he went down like a stone.'

'He was here a long time, I was kind of hoping I could buy him one day. Jeb said it was a possibility if I worked hard, did all my chores and the like.'

I got to my feet, put my hand on his back, and ruffled his hair as he walked away. I did not have words for that moment but the kid did. He turned back to me. 'I'm real glad you shot the sonofabitch that did Ben in. I thank you for that, sir.'

Again I did not know what to say so I said nothing but turned away from him and studied Main Street and the hot morning haze, trying to recall what it was like to be a youngster.

It took me just over forty minutes to reach the turn off to the Rocking J and another five to reach the gate with the lodgepole pine brand hanging from it. The same shabby, disgruntled-looking hand was on duty, sitting on the top rail, his horse tied off a few yards away. He looked at the dun horse and then at me. 'You got an appointment nobody told me about?'

'Open the gate,' I said quietly, 'just open the gate.'

'Can't do that less you got an appointment.'

'You know who I am, cowboy?'

'I don't care if you're wearing a badge, it's more than my job's worth to let you in without permission.' He fidgeted the carbine he was holding across his knees.

My jacket was folded on the buggy

seat beside me and my Colt was clearly visible. 'You know who I am.'

'I know you, you're the ranny who shot Jules Halloran.'

'Shot him dead and last afternoon I shot and killed his big brother Bobby. That's two Rocking J hands and I am just itching to make it three so you have a choice to make. You bring that Winchester and your six-gun over here and open the gate, or I am going to pull and shoot you right between your brown eyes. That is your choice, the only ones you have.'

It was an easy choice and I guess forty a month and found just wasn't worth dying for.

I rode clear up to the front door and, just like my last visit, Jimmy Keen stepped out of the shade and took hold of the horse's head.

'Jack let you in? Not like him, you must have been pretty persuasive.' He smiled the words.

'Will you tell your boss I'm here?'

'He knows, watched you coming in,

he will be out in just a minute. Won't you step down?'

'I don't think I will. Untie the dun, will you, please?'

'Suit yourself.'

'How long have you worked here, Jimmy?' I asked, killing time and knowing Weldon would not be in any hurry to see me. He'd make me wait, control the time, wait for his moment.

'I was top hand for Mr Carol, ten years or thereabouts, stayed on after the sale. Why?'

'You don't strike me as being a gunman is all.'

'I'm not, hardly ever wear one, I manage the cattle, just an old cowboy.'

He turned away from me as boot heels clumped upon the boarded porch and a beaming John Weldon made it to the top step.

'Well, what do I owe the pleasure for this visit, Mr Crow?' His soft voice, affable, innocent. Him up on the porch, me in the buggy, our heads about level.

'I brought back your horse, the one

Bobby Halloran was riding when he tried to bushwhack me yesterday out by O'Brian's spread.'

'A wild card that man, I did try to warn you.'

'Yes, you did, sir, you did that and now I am warning you, any more guns come my way I will kill them and then come out here for you.'

He stared at me for a long moment, his eyes narrowed. 'You really think you are that good, Crow?'

'I'm even better that that,' I said, clucking the horse and turning the rig back towards the main gate. The cowboy swung it open and stood to one side. I tossed him his carbine and six-gun and said, 'You are right, Jack, you may well be looking for a new job.'

* * *

Carol Creek's Main Street was pretty much deserted apart from the two town dogs and they were too hot to move or to fight and just lay, tongues lolling, on

183

the boardwalk gathering what little shade they could from the sun. It was only ten o'clock and already the heat haze was blanketing the town. Shultz appeared briefly at his store front and made a vain effort to sweep the night's dust away but quickly went back inside the relatively cool store. The only movement or sound was the chirping of the dun coloured birds that fluttered around the dried out horse droppings that littered the street's gutters.

Bob Bouchard opened his desk drawer and took out a half-empty bottle of Thomerson's special brew and topped up his own morning coffee before doing the same to the cup of Thomas Vargas, the constable who operated at the southern end of the township; the two halves split by the creek itself.

'Mite early for that, Bob,' he said quietly, 'but I guess it is late somewhere, eh?' He smiled a lovely white-toothed smile and smoothed his dark moustache to the left and right with thumb and forefinger before sipping the dark morning brew. He had a deeply pleasant voice, lyrical, especially when he was singing to the ladies.

Bouchard grinned and tapped his cup against the Mexican's. 'Salud, my friend.'

'Salud, sir. I like the morning best of all; it's so very still, I wish it will stay that way forever but I think not. I think there is big trouble coming our way.'

Bouchard nodded. 'You have seen them then, the riders.' It was not a question.

'Yes, they ride into town in twos and threes. Mostly they drift down to my end of town and give their business to the cantinas and the whorehouses but they do not make trouble for me. They were heading, I suspect, for the Rocking J ranchero.'

'Same here, no trouble, they have a drink or two, maybe a meal, but no trouble, it is almost as if they had been told not to. The small ranchers held a meeting last week here in town, invited me along with the mayor and his cronies, where they expressed their concern.'

'There has been much trouble out there for them?'

'Nothing substantial, a few cows shot up, a new fence here and there around the deeper water holes, general hazing. They cut the fence but it is back up again next day.'

'What do they expect of you?'

'I guess they expect me to do what I am paid to do, keep the peace.'

'You are one man, what happened to your tough deputy?'

Bouchard sighed. 'Part time appointment only. Crow quit as soon as he delivered the bushwhacker's pony back out to the Rocking J, dumped his badge on the desk and, as far as I can tell, lit out.'

'He coming back?'

'I really don't know, Thomas, he is kind of weird. Neither one thing or the other, a true drifter seems to me. Rolling tumbleweed. Rode out on his bay but left his war bag with the hotel clerk like he was coming back but you can never tell with a man like that.'

'He said nothing to anyone?'

'Not a word.'

'Then you really are on your own — apart from me — and I can only help within the town's boundary. Anything outside of that is county business, your business. You wired Meridian?'

'And tell Waxman what? Strangers in town, a bit of night riding out on the prairie? Send the Rangers, I'm scared? No, we will have to wait and see what develops. I may take a ride out to Weldon's place, see what he has to say.'

'Not a lot, he will not have a lot to say to you but it will let him know you are aware of the build up to what could be a bloody shooting war.'

'Could be he is waiting for something . . . '

'Or maybe someone,' Vargas interrupted.

Bouchard sighed again and sipped

some more of the coffee. 'How the hell did the two of us end up behind a badge?'

'The answer to that is easy, my friend: because we chose to.'

10

Charlie Crow

Following my delivery of Halloran's pony, I drove back to town at a leisurely pace. It was hot and the horse was sweating as was I and not only from the hot morning sun. Weldon had sounded confident, the badge did not faze him in any way. More to the contrary, I was thinking he saw it as something of a challenge.

A man is either big to begin with or he grows big somewhere along life's way. If it is there within him at the beginning then other things are likely to be in place as well, humility being one of them, as well as accepting your luck of an unearned birthright and recognizing your responsibilities to others less fortunate.

Perhaps Weldon's old man had those

things but not his son. John Junior was riding on his daddy's wealth, his heritage; it was unearned and he saw his size as the accepted part of the gift, indeed the only way to back his desire for power. He wanted the valley and the only people to stand in his way, as he saw it, were a bunch of scrub farmers, two-bit cattlemen and an over-the-hill but still capable lawman. And then, of course, the wild card rides by, a running gun, the drifter, me, Charlie Crow. It was a problem that wouldn't be solved by sitting on the fence or by gunfire and yet, in all likelihood the latter is how it would be solved and the money would be on the big man made even larger by the Sam Colt in his fist.

I checked the buggy back in and asked Luke to saddle the bay for me and to pack a gunny sack of hay and pony nuts.

'Going far, Mr Crow? Trigger is fit and ready for a ride. I took care of him personally, just like you asked me to.' It was good to see a smile back on the boy's face and maybe when this was over I could widen that smile for him.

I checked out of the hotel and asked the clerk to store my war bag for me but did not answer his query as to where I was going and how long I was going to be away, or give any assurance I would be back. I thought to say goodbye to Lily Bouchard and maybe her old man but that would require an explanation and I was in no mood to share my muddled and confused thinking with anyone or anything other than the big bay. A few minutes later I was back in my familiar range clothes, the Levis neatly repaired, the blood washed out, a long grey duster over my back and the big bay between my knees, the two of us heading northwest.

★   ★   ★

That first night out on the Texas flats, I thought I had been born again and perhaps I was. The moon hung low in the Western sky and every star in heaven was shining on Texas and me. I rolled up in my blanket with my feet, always the coldest part of me, toward the fire, and thought of Lily Bouchard back in Coral Creek and of the lonely Laura Bainbridge way back there in Cheyenne Wells. Once a coyote ventured close by, howled at the moon and, had I had the energy after a long day in the saddle, I would have gotten to my feet and howled right there alongside him.

At day break, I cooked a couple of fish I had caught in a nearby brook and washed the dirty skillet out with coarse sand and brook water. The bay had cropped the coarse grass around his tether and was eager to be up and away so we moved along quickly together, his big stride eating up the miles. The third night I was close enough to the Dubois's Arrowhead so I altered course a little and approached the run down ranch house, surprised to see smoke wisp in the early evening air from the stunted stone chimney. I rode into the yard but did not dismount.

It was much as I had last seen it, only the rocking chair had moved, rolled over on to its side. There was a single pony tied off to a rail in the broken corral. I called out to the house and waited. After a few minutes a man emerged, middle height, clean shaven, range clothes, Texas hat, denim pants, leather vest, tied down six. He was a dark-skinned man, possibly a Mexican; it was hard to tell from where I sat my horse.

'Howdy,' I said, 'just looking for a place to rest up for the night, water my horse is all, you have any objections?'

'Light down, be glad of the company, this place gives me the damn creeps.' His smile was genuine.

'I'll see to my horse then join you. I've got bacon, beans and fresh eggs, am happy to share them.'

'Save them, I got jackrabbit stew that will be about ready by the time you put up your animal.'

I lead the pony out of the corral and put it and the bay up in what was left of the barn and gave them water and food, rubbed it down and said goodnight to Trigger, thinking of Luke back in Coral Creek.

The man did not offer his name and I did not give mine. We would eat, sleep and in all likelihood, never meet again so names were not needed. His stew was excellent and with our coffee and after dinner smokes, I offered him a slug of whiskey purchased from Thomerson before I left town, in case of snake bite I had told him.

'I put your pony in the barn, I think it's going to blow later.' The man nodded his thanks but did not look up from studying the glowing end of his stogie. 'You say this place gives you the creeps?'

'There's no wind or breeze but I swear that old chair was rocking shortly before you rode in, is why I put it on its side, oh, and there is an unmarked grave at the back of the barn. Sure enough weird.'

'I wonder who lived here,' I said, innocently.

'Or who died here more like,' he offered with a shudder.

'Where you headed?' I asked, there was no reason not to.

'Some small burg called Carol Creek, about two or three days' ride from here. Some trouble brewing, hiring guns, top dollar.' He eyed my Colt. 'You interested?'

'I would think twice about that,' I said, 'they have a regular lawman.'

'So I hear tell, from some long old over the hill coot.'

'Your life but I would think on it some, I have just come through there, too hot for me. That old coot got himself a running gun for a deputy, already killed three gunnies from up north. Maybe you have heard of him, the deputy's name, Charlie Crow.'

'*The* Charlie Crow? Jesus, I didn't know that. Thanks. I think I will head on down to the flats and tell the men I was aiming to team up with and then move on back north, maybe Louisiana. Jesus, I wonder if Billy Joe knows Crow is down there waiting for him.'

'Billy Joe Watts?' Just saying the words out loud hurt me. I see him often but I never speak his name out loud. I see him looking up at me with those dead blue eyes, telling me he will be seeing me sometime, someday, somewhere further down the line.

'Yeah, Billy Joe Watts thinks he's the original Billy the Kid, a sure enough weird hombre. Goddamn it, a long wasted ride, glad I ran into you. Hell, I'm turning in. I'm leaving early so if you are not up when I leave, thanks for the hooch, good stuff.'

I rolled a smoke and watched him stoke up the stove and then roll into his blankets. Outside, the north wind had suddenly risen as it can in Texas, seemingly out of the ground, blowing dust and tumbleweed across the yard. I shuttered up the window as best I could and settled into my own blanket roll with my saddle for a pillow. The barn was sturdy so the horses would be safe and well out of it. It took me a long time to find relief and only then when Billy Joe Watts was out of sight and out of mind, and the howling wind like some demonic lullaby lured me into a dreamless sleep.

When I rolled out of my blanket in the morning, my companion had already left. I cooked some breakfast and wandered out to the barn, fed the bay and searched the dark corners of the barn until I found a rusted running iron. I built a small but hot fire close by the old graveside and spent an hour or so heating and reheating the iron, and burning Sam Dubois's name into the sun bleached marker. The smoke smelled clean and I hoped Hannah would have approved, though I doubted it. In any event, it did not really matter; it was simply another trail ended.

* * *

Meridian was much as I expected it to be, maybe bigger, bawdier and more modern than Coral Creek thanks to the railroad. The bustling Main Street was free of ruts, and was lamp lit from one end to the other. The boardwalk was covered end to end and boasted a barber shop, gun shop, two general stores, several saloons and cafes, two billiard halls, a livery, milliner, saddle maker and a large bank. For law, there was the splendid county hall with its flag pole draped with the Lone Star flag and a statue of a civil war soldier out front. There was also a US Marshal's office, a land office next door to a white clapboard building with a doctor's shingle squeaking in the breeze.

I walked the bay to the livery, where the stable-hand told me that it would be a dollar a night with feed. Next I checked into the smaller of the three hotels at a dollar a night, plus an extra buck for a bath. I had a quick meal which was also a dollar a throw, it was a one dollar kind of town and as my resources were fairly limited, I thought to get out of there as soon as possible.

First thing after the dollar breakfast, I walked the Main Street, thinking. I could speak with Sheriff Waxman but that seemed a little underhanded, going to Bouchard's boss without clearing it with Bouchard first. I was standing there on the boardwalk, rolling a quirly from the dust of my tobacco sack when US Marshal Wally Dade brushed past me and went into his office. I followed him in.

'Can I help you?'

His voice was raspy, tobacco stained. A small man dressed in a black wool suit neatly brushed and pressed, there was no sign of his badge or a gun so I guessed that the former was pinned to his vest and the gun hidden in a shoulder rig. He settled himself on the edge of his polished wood desk and indicated a round backed chair for me.

'Take the weight off.' He smiled. 'Coffee?'

'Will it cost me a dollar?' I asked,

returning his grin.

'New in town, huh? Well, there was a time you could get a haircut and shave for two bits, now it will cost you a buck and a half. No, coffee here is on the government.' He walked over to the potbellied stove, put a cloth on the handle of the blackened coffee pot and filled two tin cups. 'Sugar?'

I nodded. 'A couple if you can spare them.'

'Sweet tooth, huh? Man after my own heart. What brings you to me this one goddamned hot morning?' He was known in the service as Wally 'God-damned' Dade, a sobriquet rightly earned for his constant use of the word. 'Say, haven't I seen you somewhere before, have we ever met?'

'Not directly,' I said, remembering that afternoon on the Arizona line when I had spooked his horse but I thought it best not to own up to that encounter. 'But we may have crossed trails, have mutual friends maybe.'

He looked puzzled and he studied me

while sipping the scalding Joe. Finally he said, 'Mutual friends, you say? How are you called?'

It was a quaint way of putting it. 'Charlie Crow,' I said, and waited.

He thought for a moment. 'Charlie Crow, eh, of course, you rode with Harry Boudine under a Wyoming warrant some time back, also with Earp, I believe. Boudine spoke well of you; Wyatt, he rarely spoke well of anyone, though.'

I nodded. 'How is Harry?'

'Still behind a badge but like me, mostly past it. He was here for a spell. So, what can I do for you? You come to pick up your mail?'

'Excuse me?'

'Collect your mail. Got a letter here somewhere for you, came a couple of weeks ago.' He rummaged through a wad of letters and picked out one, read it briefly and passed it to me. 'Return address is Cheyenne Wells, Wyoming.'

I looked at it briefly, folded it

unopened and put it in my jacket pocket.

'Not going to read it, it sure smells nice.' A hint of a smile.

'Thanks, Marshal, but that's not what I came here for.' In the cool of that office I outlined as clearly as I could my thoughts on events in Carol Creek, where I thought they might lead and the vulnerability of Robert Bouchard and the open aggression of John Weldon.

He listened patiently. 'Refill?'

'Thank you.' I handed him my empty cup, surprised at how long it had taken me to outline events that had happened so suddenly.

'You spoken to Sheriff Waxman yet?'

'No, and I don't intend to, that would be disloyal of me. Bouchard has treated me squarely and I do not intend to make out he is not up to doing his job.'

'You came to me, though. Is there a difference?'

'A big one. He is county law, you are

federal. In Johnson County the war was only over when the army moved in at, I guess, the behest of the Marshal's Office in Cheyenne.'

'You think I should saddle up and ride down there on just your supposition that there is going to be mayhem and a range war? Boudine said you were smart, so my guess is that you didn't really believe that was going to happen and anyway, I have to be in court in Wichita day after tomorrow and that alone is going to be a rush. Goddamn it, I got one year to run and this is my last stint of four, it was going to be a quiet fishing and hunting kind of a year and then you show up.'

We both sat there in silence, the only sound the buzzing of a bluebottle fly trapped behind the drawn window blind.

Dade broke the silence, smiled knowingly and said, 'Of course, there is a way, Crow, and I'm guessing this is the way you had in mind.'

He slid off the desk and went around

behind it, dumped his slight frame into the big chair and opening a side drawer, took out a leather folder and opened it. He looked at me long and hard then, taking up a pen and dipping it in the inkwell, he wrote on the pad, blotted it, tore out the page and folding it, placed it on the desk between us.

'Harry Boudine is my one and best friend, I would trust his judgement with my life and on several occasions have done just that. You know what that is?' He indicated the folded paper. 'Of course you do, it's what you hoped for but were too goddamned coy to ask for outright.'

'It's a warrant,' I said, 'I've had one before.'

'You are goddamned right it is. A Deputy US Marshal's warrant issued by my hand on behalf of the US Attorney's office and backed by the President of these United States, you serve it well.' He reached back into the drawer and pulled out a black leather wallet, opened it and tossed it beside the paper. 'Sometimes it is best to keep that badge in your pocket and wear it when you need to, bit like a gun really. Just knowing you have it and can use it if you have to is sometimes enough.'

There was no need for more words on the subject of Carol County. I got to my feet, put the paper and the badge holder into my shirt pocket.

'Thanks, Marshal, appreciated, I won't let you down. Say hello to Harry for me and remind him I'm still carrying lead from Cheyenne, he will understand. Tell him I'm sorry I missed him here.'

We shook hands and I stepped out into the sunlight.

'Oh, one other thing, Crow, forty a month goes with the job and any bounty you collect, so you can afford to get a bath and a shave before you ride out; it looks and smells like you could do with both.'

I did not turn around and he did not expect me to.

11

Distant Thunder

Robert Bouchard checked his mail while finishing his morning coffee, just the usual flyers and routine letters from the County Seat in Meridian. He checked the loads and action of his short barrelled Colt and slipped it back into its shoulder holster, an automatic reflex for any lawman, no point in carrying a gun that would not perform. Outside, he heard the buggy he had ordered from the stable, the horse snorting irritably, perhaps for having been dragged out of the cool stable interior. Luke stepped down and held the animal's head while the sheriff climbed aboard.

'You going far, Sheriff?'

'No, son, just out to the Rocking J. I will be back just after noon I guess.'

'You heard from Mr Crow, sir?'

'No again, Luke, not a word.' He snapped the reins and left the crest-fallen boy standing in the dusty street. 'Damn Crow,' he muttered, 'everyone wants to know where the hell he is.'

He did not push the horse, rather, he let it keep to a steady trot until he reached the turn off then he slowed it to a walk and stopped by the gate, waiting for the cowhand on duty to open it. The man walked over to the buggy. 'You got an appointment, mister?'

'I don't need one.' He let his jacket fall open, pointed to the star. 'County business is all.'

'Guess that will be OK then.' The man released the catch and the gate swung open.

The buggy pulled to a halt by the main door and the ever present Jimmy Keen stepped down from the porch and took the animal's head. 'Morning, Sheriff, the boss will be out directly, he's expecting you.'

'How did he know it was me?'

Keen grinned. 'We got a man on the roof with a scope, can't be too careful these days.'

Weldon thumped out on to the porch and nodded to Bouchard. The man was irritable, not his usual welcoming self and he did not make an offer for the visitor to step down.

'What can I do for you, Bouchard? I've got no time for idle chatter this morning.'

'Neither have I, John. Just a courtesy call to let you know I am aware of the build-up of dubious looking cowhands you are signing on these days and to tell you if there is any trouble in the county from them, I will hold you and the Rocking J responsible.'

'You are telling me what?'

'I think you get my drift, sir.'

'Well, you get mine, Bouchard. You are a spent force in this county, you're old, your gunfighter quit on you and was smart enough to hightail it north and maybe you should do the same.

One way or another, this is going to be my valley. You and those scrub ranchers stand in my way and I will ride right over you all. On the other hand, you stand by me and you could be wearing Waxman's badge come the next election.'

Bouchard sighed deeply, shook his head and worked the reins, turning the horse's head back towards the gate. About a mile from town, he stopped, took a deep pull at the warm water in his canteen and lit a stogie.

Weldon was waiting to see if there was going to be any real opposition to his taking over the valley and possibly waiting for fresh troops but he would not wait long. Still no point in wiring Waxman; he was on his own, always had been, he guessed, that was the way of the badge.

He dogged the stogie between thumb and forefinger and pushed the buggy on, driving right through town and up to the livery doors. Luke was there waiting, he held the halter while

Bouchard climbed down, his back aching, tired and weary through to the very bone. He gave the boy a quarter, thanked him and walked back to his office. He had tried, done his best and now it was up to Weldon. If he made a move then it would be a different matter but until then there was little he could do. Well, he thought, there was always one thing he could do, take a nap. He poured himself a generous shot of Thomerson's brew, drank it slowly then set back in his chair. Eyelids heavy, he slept through the hot afternoon.

As the day cooled, the two town dogs remembered their quarrel of the night before and set to with their barking and snarling, a fight halted by Shultz tossing a bucket of cold water on them. The noise awakened Bouchard but it was more than the racket that had disturbed him and grunting, he opened his eyes as a tall shadow fell across him, blotting out the dusty, pale sunlight seeping in through the open door. He slowly straightened, his hand automatically moving towards his holstered Colt, but then he paused and stared as the man entered the small room.

'Where the hell have you been, Crow? We've been looking all over for you.'

*   *   *

Jesus O'Brian and the dog worked the small herd of cattle out of the brush corral he had built to hold them as he gathered them together from the scrub brush on the northern end of his property. Maybe thirty head, more than enough for one cowman to handle for even the short drive back to the larger holding ground fenced off to the east of the ranch house. They were wild, mostly unbranded and unhappy about being worked by a man on a horse with a snappy dog riding to his heel.

O'Brian was not an ambitious man but he loved the life he led. He earned just about enough from the cattle and the hooch he ran on the side from his well-hidden still in the rocky, stream fed arroyo, was tucked away on government land and an easy wagon ride from the house. The still would be a concern if the stream dried up but he thought that unlikely and anyway, the rain would come soon. So far his water hole was running clear and although the run off had been dammed by a couple of Rocking J hands, it took but an hour to clear it. That would be tomorrow's problem; today he was a cowhand and enjoying the work.

He was happy, his wife was happy, his children fed and healthy and well tutored by the woman he had chosen, or had she chosen him? Sometimes he thought it might well be the latter and it did not matter as they were a team. He was respected and looked upon as the spokesman for the small ranchers that stood in John Weldon's way. He liked that, enjoyed the respect that they showed him.

He was thinking those things, wondering if he should find some shade for a pull at his canteen, maybe roll a smoke and let the dog take care of the cattle when the 30.30 round knocked him out of the saddle and on to the hard, dry earth. He lay there listening to the barking of the dog and the bellowing cattle as one by one, they too fell under the guns of the hidden carbines.

★   ★   ★

It was early evening and Gloria O'Brian drove the buck-board into Carol Creek like a woman possessed; she swore at the horses, cracking the whip above their heads and screaming for help as she hauled the animals to a jerking halt in front of the sheriff's office. Bouchard stumbled out of the doorway, his Colt in his hand and stared up at the woman.

'Gloria, what the hell . . . ?'

'Jesus has been shot. Get Doc Owens, it's real bad, we need help now, right now.'

Lily Bouchard ran past her father, and climbed up on to the buckboard, taking the situation at a glance and yelling over her shoulder, 'Dad, get the doc and get someone to help with these poor kids.'

Then Owens was up there with her, pushing her to one side as she handed the crying, frightened O'Brian children down to ready, gentle hands. A warm breeze rustled down Main Street, flickering the oil lamps, making long shadows on the boardwalk as the doctor and the storekeeper Shultz carried the injured Jesus O'Brian into Doc Owens's office, laying him gently on to a long white table, and all the while Gloria O'Brian held the man's bloody hand and crooned reassuring words to him, a reassurance she did not feel.

An hour later, Doc Owens walked into the sheriff's dimly lit office. Tired and white-faced, he slumped into the round-backed chair set in front of Bouchard's desk and gladly took the

214

glass of Thomerson's brew offered to him.

Without waiting to be asked he said quietly, 'It's a bad one, Bob, but he might make it. A weaker man, no, but a tough old Irishman like that with a wife as feisty as all outdoors? Yes, he could make it but it will be his and God's doing, not mine.'

Bouchard turned to the shadowy figure of Charlie Crow, the tall man standing by the window, staring out into the night.

'O'Brian's not the only one who was hit last night, I just heard a settler was shot and killed in the north end of the canyon, up near Kiowa Pass. His house was burned down and stock run off or killed.'

'So it begins,' said Crow quietly.

'It began the day John Weldon bought the Rocking J.'

'No,' said Crow, 'it began the day John Weldon was born.'

'Can I tempt you back behind a badge, Crow?'

The tall man turned to face the room. 'No, thanks, Bob, I already have one.' He pulled the black leather badge holder from his shirt pocket, flipped it open and tossed it on to Bouchard's desk.

The old lawman stared at the star inset in the centre of the silver shield and turned to Crow; there were a lot of things he wanted to ask, to say, but instead he smiled and offered only, 'You sure do get around, Charlie Crow.'

'You want my help?'

'Hell, man, I need your help, that badge carries more weight than my star and besides, the nester was on federal land that gives you point on this one.'

'You OK with that, Bob?'

'More than OK.'

12

John H. Weldon

John Weldon surveyed the bits and working pieces of the Smith and Wesson Schofield single action pistol spread carefully over an old newspaper on his large desk. He liked the pistol and figured the seven inch barrel was an advantage as far as range and accuracy were concerned, and superior to the US Army Colt with its six inch barrel. Not that he thought himself as anything of a gunfighter but he could shoot that pistol straight and he liked to wear it around the ranch, part of his perceived self, his image. He sipped at the whiskey over ice Maria had poured for him. There was a ring as the bell set on the outside of the main door signalled an unexpected visitor. He listened as Maria drifted silently past him to the door, wondering who was calling.

'Mr Keen wishes to speak with you, Señor.' She always addressed him formally, even on the regular visits to his bed to fulfil the duties his wife no longer offered.

'Show him in, Maria, and bring another glass.'

Keen carefully wiped his boots on the door mat, crossed the room and settled in the chair offered him, declining the drink and asking if it was OK to smoke. Weldon nodded and slid a carved box toward his foreman, flipping the lid to reveal a layer of tailor-made cigarettes. Again, Keen declined the offer and pulled the sack of Durham from his shirt pocket and carefully rolled a smoke.

'What's on your mind, Jimmy?'

Keen studied the dismantled pistol for a long moment. 'I guess that is, boss.' He nodded toward the pistol. 'There seems to be more gunhands around here than cowhands at the moment.'

Weldon smiled, irritated but not showing it. Keen was a dinosaur, a man who only drank on a Saturday night, who preferred dusty rolling tobacco from a linen sack to a fine Virginia tobacco, machine rolled, tailor-made cigarette. A man who never wore a pistol. An ageing man, fit now but inevitably on the decline, his years just beginning to show, the broken bones of a bronc busting youth, destined to die in the saddle on some lonely trail and be buried beside that trail in a shallow, unmarked grave without anything to show of his passing, of his years of hard work. The big man found such a life unimaginable, unacceptable, the old cowboy unfathomable.

'You ever wear a piece, Jimmy?' Weldon began gathering the Schofield together, clicking the bits so as they fitted snugly into one another. The smell of gun oil was released as metal bonded to metal, the assembly formed the whole as he worked the mechanism.

'No, sir, only very rarely, never had

the need. Heavy for one thing and a pistol will not do anything a saddle gun cannot do as well or even better.'

'The men coming in here, they bother you?'

'They are not cattlemen, they have no desire to work and even if they did, I don't need them. We have enough good riders to take care of a bigger herd than we already have so I guess they are here for another reason, a reason I want no part of.' Keen spoke the words quietly, almost offhanded, simply stating a fact, pulling gently on his quirly and blowing the smoke to one side, watching it drift across the room and out of the open window.

'Fair enough, Jimmy, I will not involve you in any of this. You just work the ranch as always and I will take care of the new men. It will all be over in a couple of days and we can get back to normal. That be fair enough with you?'

Keen got to his feet and stubbed the quirly in the pristine ashtray. 'I am not too sure that it will be over in a few days, Mr Weldon, I hear Charlie Crow is back in Carol Creek.'

Weldon did not show either the surprise or the irritation he felt at that news, he simply smiled and walked his foreman to the door.

'Let me worry about that. Goodnight to you, Jimmy, and thanks for letting me know how you feel.' Keen only nodded and Weldon closed the door behind him, turning to meet Josie as she stepped into the room and poured herself a whiskey in the glass Keen had declined.

'When this is over you need to fire that man and find one with some balls.'

'You were listening?'

'Someone has to take care of you and what the hell are you fooling around with that gun for? We have men to do that for us.'

'Yes, we have but not the right man yet.'

Weldon took a cigarette from the box and fired it with a blue top match, inhaling the smoke, enjoying the pain of the sudden burn, blowing the smoke clear and sipping the whiskey, staring at Josie over the rim of the glass. He did not know her now, she was not the Texas girl he had married; there was no closeness, no warmth. He let her think she ruled the roost, it suited him and in some strange way, he enjoyed her pleasure at the power she believed she had over him. A dreg of the love and respect they had once shared now burned out like the smouldering brown paper quirly Jimmy Keen had left in the ash tray. She no longer served him as a wife in any way, in any caring way. She no longer shared his bed and he knew she was aware of his liaison with Maria and the fact that it did not bother her did not bother him.

'And when will this mystery man arrive so we can get this mess cleared?' She stared at him, waiting for an answer.

'He will be in Carol Creek this evening, check out the lay of the land for himself and then head out here. He has maybe three riders with him and with those we have here already, it should be easy.'

'Did you know Charlie Crow was back in the game?'

'It makes no difference, in fact it will help my man make up his mind.'

'And the name of this man?'

'Billy Joe Watts, it is almost too perfect.'

'What do you mean? What the hell is going on with you?'

'I sent for Billy Joe because he and Crow have a history, they go back a piece, had some sort of falling out. I don't know the details, I am not sure anyone does but it is there nevertheless. They say Billy Joe has the deadeye on Crow. Crow has kept his distance, maybe running scared, maybe just some superstition he has; gunfighters are like that. They live in the shadows, they are drifters and they do think a great deal about their mortality. Perhaps too much living on the edge, within reach of the Reaper, a trigger pull away and that's the job.'

'How come you know so much about it?' There was a curiosity in her voice; he thought for a moment she was actually interested in something he said but doubted that was the motivation behind the question.

'I know men, Josie, and unlike you, I respect them. Even men like Jimmy Keen and Billy Joe Watts and especially men like Charlie Crow, put those two together in some Roman arena, watch them fight to the death. A puppet master, he who pays the piper never loses as long as he knows the tune he is calling.' He laughed, turned his back on her and went again to the table and the Smith & Wesson Schofield he would not have to use but would have ready just in case.

13

Billy Joe Watts

'Evening , Charlie, it's been a while.'

I did not look up immediately, knowing who it was even as his shadow fell across my table in the Longhorn Saloon, darkening the page of the newspaper I was reading. I carefully folded the page and raised my head. He had not changed much in the nine or so months since we had parted. Hair a little shorter, maybe a little fuller in the clean shaven face, a tan Montana peaked hat riding a little high on his head and a dusty dark wool suit had replaced the worn range clothes he had been wearing when I had last seen him. He was sporting a two gun rig, something you did not see every day, guns are heavy and if you could not get the job done with one, then most figured a second would be of little use to you.

'Hello, Billy,' I said, 'it has been a while, a year maybe?'

'Getting on for that.'

'You keeping well?'

'Better than most.'

'You're packing a lot of iron.'

'Mostly just for show, Charlie, I get it done with one but two looks better.'

'Impressive.'

'That's the point. Mind if I sit down?'

'Free country last time I heard.'

He pulled out the chair opposite me, sat down and nodded to one of the four men with him. The quartet wore dark suits under their dusters and low slung, tied down holstered pistols.

'Get yourselves a drink at the bar, boys, and send a bottle over to the table. I need to talk to my old bunky here.' The men moved away obediently.

'Riding through?'

'Maybe yes and maybe no, that depends on a lot of things, Charlie.' He grinned and nodded at the badge on my vest. 'A lawman? Now that is something to see. Job pay well?'

'It has its advantages.' We were fencing. He did not turn around or acknowledge in any way the dark suited man who brought a bottle to the table, set a glass beside it and moved back to the bar.

'What is it? A deputy sheriff, I heard.'

'Look again, Billy Joe.' I let my jacket fall clear of the badge and he leaned forward, nodded and settled back in his chair, a puzzled look on his young face. He poured a generous drink and topped up my empty glass. 'A Deputy US Marshal, now that is something to think about.' He raised his glass. 'To old times, old trails.'

There was no point in not doing so; I raised my glass, tapped it against his. 'To old times, Billy Joe, the good ones that is.'

He chuckled. 'All old times are good to someone.' There was slight edge to his voice and the smile had vanished.

He leaned forward. 'You know why we are here, Charlie, you going to make it difficult for us?'

'You riding for the Rocking J?'

'That's the intention, just on our way out there — big I understand — see if we can't come to an agreement about how much we are worth.' He paused. 'Yes, sir, just like the good old times.'

He refilled his glass and hovered the bottle over mine but I covered the glass with my hand and shook my head. He tossed back his drink and nodded to the four men, who emptied their glasses and without a word, walked across the room and out of the swing doors, their spurs clinking, dust raised from the cracked boards drifting into the air and catching the rays of the sun like speckled arrows.

'Be seeing you then, I guess, one way or another.' He got to his feet, the young smile returning to his narrow mouth but never reaching the pale eyes.

I nodded and watched him, light on his feet, hardly a sound as he moved to the door. He paused and I thought he was going to turn around but he did not, maybe he believed all that needed to be said had been said and then he was gone. I heard the creak of saddle leather and the snorting of a horse and then they were all gone.

★   ★   ★

The room was wreathed in tobacco smoke drifting across the high ceiling and vanishing through the open windows and out into the darkened evening. Billy Joe felt comfortable in the big house, leaning against the cold stone fireplace, sipping fine whiskey and smoking a store bought cigarette, drawing in deeply without getting flakes of dry Durham latched on to his tongue, blowing the hot tobacco smoke out through his nostrils and flipping the grey ash into the blackened grate and on to the cold ashes of the previous night's fire.

There were several men in the room

apart from the four who rode with him. His four man army stood out and apart from the others, dressed in black from hats to boots, quietly talking amongst themselves, at ease, smoking, rattling the ice in their glasses. A dark comparison to the other new Rocking J hands who were noisy, unkempt, long-haired, in dusty range clothes, wore low slung Colts, were ill at ease with the crystal glasses and happy with their cheap stogies and thin rolled cigarettes.

The murmuring of their combined voices suddenly stilled as John H. Weldon walked into the room, accompanied by his wife, Josie. The men removed their hats and dogged their cigarettes, shifted their feet awkwardly, waiting.

Weldon sought out Billy Joe Watts who had not moved from his place by the fire and walked over to him, hand extended. The men shook hands, sizing each other up; two cockerels, one barnyard.

'Welcome to the Rocking J, Mr Watts.'

'Happy to be here and I am called Billy, the mister makes me sound old.'

'That seems to be a general feeling around here and John is fine by me.' He smiled. 'Billy, I would like you to meet my wife, Josie.'

'Pleased to meet you, ma'am.'

'Josie, please.' She gave him the same smile she had given Crow only a few weeks before.

'Pretty name, seems like we are all friends around here already.' The soft voice, the cold smile that creased his lips and never reached his pale eyes, something that Weldon noticed and wondered about.

'Billy,' Weldon lowered his voice, 'I am going to address the men in general terms but I wish to speak with you in private. I didn't ask you here tonight to ride over some nesters and two by four ranchers, but that will be between me and your men. I will be brief and when I have finished, you and I will retire with that bottle to my private office. That OK with you?'

Billy Joe nodded. 'Your show, John.'

Weldon moved to the centre of the room and banged his fist down hard on the polished table. 'Your attention, please. Welcome to you all, some I have already met and the others I will in due course. You are being paid for your expertise with firearms and to follow my instructions to the letter, no deviations whatsoever.

'In a few days from now, we will ride and clear this lovely valley of the filth of the squatters and the thieving ranchers who steal my water and my cattle. But first we have to dampen down the ardour of the local law enforcement officers, an over-the-hill sheriff and a two-bit washed up gunslinger who has outlived his reputation and hides behind a deputy US marshal's badge. When they have been dealt with and the ranchers driven out, you will be paid and can melt across the border. The gold in your pokes will keep you happy until it is safe for you to drift back into Texas.

'I do not expect any comeback from the law once this is over, but should there be, I will take that on board here at the Rocking J; I have good friends at the county seat.' He smiled, 'It pays to be sure you have good friends before setting out on such a venture as this. Now, there are smokes and whiskey aplenty, and help yourselves to the food which will be on the table shortly. Thank you, gentlemen.' He turned to Billy Joe Watts, nodding toward the office and made his own way there, picking up a bottle and three glasses on the way.

* * *

John Weldon was relaxed; he flopped down into his big, polished leather chair and indicated that Billy Joe take the seat opposite while Josie Weldon chose an upright padded one just to the left of the door. Weldon filled three whiskey glasses; Billy Joe took one but the woman declined with a slight nod of the head.

'Was that about what you expected, Billy?'

The young gunman did not answer right away, sipping his whiskey, thinking it through. 'About. I know you would not have asked me and my men here to deal with a bunch of squatters, that riff raff you have out there could and will do that for you. You have something else for us and that something will cost you a whole lot more than what those gunnies are getting. That about right?'

'More than about, Billy, you are dead right. A couple of those men will help you with your end, you probably know them already. Joe Butcher and Big Red Rivers — he rode in with you — and the other one they call Latigo. All three are top gunhands but the others are for show now and later to do the night riding. I did have three more but an old friend of yours, Charlie Crow, got himself a badge and took them out early on. Of course I use the term old friend loosely, although I hear you have met somewhere along the road.'

'You know damn well I have, else you wouldn't have got me down here.'

The cold smile over the rim of the glass chilled Weldon. 'True enough, Billy.'

'Good old righteous Charlie Crow and I go back a couple of years. I had a parlay with him today in your town, seems he is the deputy US marshal here and he was not too happy to see me, said I was packing too much iron.' He chuckled. 'That badge sure enough makes a fine target, but note this, John, I will not come at him from a dark alley. I want him to know we are coming hard, and it will have to be on Main Street so folk can see it was a fair fight, an old grudge. I don't want the federal law dogging my tracks the rest of my life after I cut him down and I tell you this also, the lead I use will not come cheap.'

'How much is not cheap?' Josie

Weldon rose from her seat and stood in front of Billy Joe Watts, staring down at him and offering the same cold smile he offered to others, all lips and no eyes.

Billy stared right back up at her and for just a moment the smile did, very briefly, reach his pale eyes and just as quickly faded. 'A thousand for Crow and $500 for the sheriff — that's just for me, plus $500 for each of my four men. Anyone else we take out is for free. With travelling money let's call that a round $5,000 in US gold.'

'That's an awful lot of money for one night's work, Billy; you sure you can cut it with Charlie Crow?' She took a cigarette from the box and waited for him to light it for her. He fired a blue top with his thumb and reached up, lighting the cigarette. She held his gaze with her own, inhaled and blew the smoke clear above his head. 'They say you have the deadeye on him, is that a fact or saloon talk?'

'Probably a little of both, Josie.'

She laughed and turned back to her

chair but did not sit down, instead she reached for the door handle, turning only briefly to address Weldon. 'Pay the man, John, let's get this done.' She closed the door quietly behind her.

14

Showdown

I was eating my steak supper at The Green Frog and reading the Meridian newspaper brought in on the afternoon stage when the gate keeping cowboy from the Rocking J I knew only as Jack waltzed in through the open doorway, looked nervously around and made his way over to my table. It was still early evening and the place was pretty much deserted, just as I liked it. He stood by the table, fidgeting his dusty boots with each movement accompanied by the rattle of his spurs. I looked up and waited, watching as he licked his lips.

'Got something on your mind there, Jack? Looking for work, maybe?'

'I didn't get fired, Mr Crow, boss said you would likely have shot me dead had I not let you in.'

'You think I would have done that, Jack, shot you dead?'

'No, sir.'

'Good, now what can I do for you today, seeing as I haven't shot anyone since breakfast?'

The humour was lost on the man. 'Mr Weldon asked me to tell you he was bringing some men into town tomorrow near sundown. You and the sheriff got until then to move the nesters out of the valley peaceful like or he is going to move you and then them out unpeaceful like.'

I pushed my plate away, wiped my lips with the napkin and carefully folded the newspaper before returning my attention to the nervous cowboy. 'He said that, did he, that's exactly what he said?'

'Yes, sir, more or less exactly that.'

'And you, Jack, will you be riding into town with him tomorrow?'

'No, sir, I'm not a gunman, just a working cowboy like Jimmy Keen is all.' He stepped back, knocking over a chair, then he picked it up and opened his coat. 'See, I don't even pack.'

'Well, you get this right, Jack, more or less. You tell John Weldon the small ranchers and settlers in this valley are now under federal protection and if anything happens to any one of them, I will slam his backside in jail along with anyone who chooses to ride with him and that includes the man who shot Jesus O'Brian. Can you remember that, Jack, more or less?'

★   ★   ★

'They will come and they will come in hard,' I said, aiming the words directly at Bouchard, my voice unnecessarily tough, trying to make a point and hoping they were as committed as myself.

But there was a nagging doubt. It really wasn't my fight and win, lose or draw, the end would eventually be the same; if it wasn't Weldon today it would as like or not be someone else down the line. The small ranchers were being eased out all over the West, the big spreads being gobbled up as investments by men in the East who never had the desire, and in all probability never would have, to visit their acquisitions, figures in a ledger, a bank account measured by the price of beef and not the sweat and blood of the men who produced that meat.

I thought of the letter from Cheyenne Wells, I had read it many times. Laura Bainbridge was hoping I would be back before the end of the fall, maybe the winter for a few days at the line shack. I could almost hear her laughter at that. She had tamed a crow, she fed it and in return it brought her small gifts, coloured glass shards, buttons, pebbles and once, a used orange shotgun shell. She called it Charlie and had told it about me, the real Crow in her life.

Why the hell did I not just saddle up and ride, dump the badge and the life? I tried not to think about that or of Cheyenne Wells but she was there in the back of my mind all through the following hours.

The office was stuffy and smoke-filled. I opened the window, enjoying the gentle breeze that wafted in and, like magic, cleared the air. I stared out into the deserted street; word travels fast in a small town and the good citizens of Carol Creek had gone to ground so I very much doubted they would emerge again until the final bell tolled either over the bodies of the ambitious and wealthy John H. Weldon and his hired guns or the three lawmen who would, in all probability, die poor, earning no more than the fifty or so dollars a month due to them for giving their lives. But it would not come to that, it never had for me and I believed, foolishly perhaps, that it never would.

Once his gun was in his hand, I knew Bouchard could handle his end and although I did not know the Mexican Town constable Vargas, he seemed at home with a sawed off double barrelled shotgun, his weapon of choice. He smiled as he checked each round by shaking it near his ear, happy with the sound of the double ought buck lead balls rattling inside. He loaded his long jacket pockets with shells, lit himself another stogie from the end of the last one and sipped at the last of Thomerson's special brew.

'When do you think they will hit, Crow?' Bouchard asked quietly.

'Just before sunset when the sun is low and to their backs, they will ride in from the west, hoping for an advantage.' I thought for a moment, adding, 'But then again it might not happen like that.'

The idea suddenly struck me that might not be the play Weldon had in mind. He had chosen Billy Joe Watts carefully, selected him for a reason and that reason had to be me. He maybe knew we had history and if that was the case, if it was in Billy Joe's hands, the kid would not want it to play out that way. Maybe, just maybe he would come for me himself, call me out. If I faded him, Weldon could call in his heavies but if the kid beat me, then it was job over, he could take him down and come out of the mess clean and possibly with little interference from Meridian. It was a thought I shared with the two men.

Range wars happen but this was no Johnson County. Carol Creek was a little valley, a patch of land part Mexican and part American, a patch of land with its back to the Rio Grande. If whatever happened here happened real quick, nothing much would be gained by the financially stretched US Government taking too much of an interest, an interest that might prove costly and stir up resentment come election time. Another maybe was that Weldon was smarter than I had given him credit for or then again, maybe it was Josie who was more savvy than both of us.

At 5.30 I sent Vargas across the street to the livery and told him not to shoot until I did. He nodded, offered me his hand and I took it.

'Good luck, Marshal.' He smiled and

left, striding purposefully across the street, dumping his spent stogie in the horse trough.

'Where do you want me, Crow?'

'Here will do fine, Bob. Keep as low as you can when the shooting starts, don't make an easy target of yourself and you might find a rifle better than a handgun but that is up to you. Is Lily OK with this?'

'It's what I do, she knows that.'

'Where is she?'

'With Susan at The Green Frog, says she will have supper waiting for us.'

They rode in at 5.45. Billy Joe Watts, his four gunmen and three of the heavies from the Rocking J. I recognized the one they called Red Rivers, the man I had met out at the Dubois spread, the man frightened of a rocking chair, the other one I knew only as Latigo, a breed I had seen in Thomerson's place on a number of occasions. I did not know the third man. There was no sign of Weldon. We watched as they tied their horses outside the hotel and then moved across the street, careful to put the animals out of danger in case they were needed for a quick getaway. Billy Joe's thinking there, I guessed.

Then it played out as I suspected.

Billy Joe Watts moved up the street alone towards the jailhouse while his men held back, almost loitering, seemingly indifferent to the mayhem likely to follow, whatever the outcome.

Billy Joe paused, standing tall, his weight on his right hip, about thirty yards out, a good range for my Colt. 'You coming out or what, Marshal?' That mean smile that never reached his eyes, the thought that had dogged my nights for so long.

I stepped out of the doorway and down off the sidewalk and on to the street. 'You sure you want it this way, Billy? Not too late to ride out.'

'You are damned wrong, it is too late.' But the words did not come from the mouth of Billy Joe Watts, it was a red-faced Weldon emerging from the alleyway next to the saloon, a long barrelled Schofield stretched out, straight armed and aimed at me. I took in two things very quickly, the look of anger and absolute dismay on the face of Billy Joe as he half turned to face the big rancher and the hesitation in the movement of his right hand. Faced between the threat from a man in two minds as to whether or not to make a play and one with a gun pointed at me, I chose. I pulled and shot Weldon, hitting him hard in the shoulder, on the bone and spinning him around. The Smith dumped its capped round into the dust by my left boot.

Then all hell broke loose as the men behind Billy thought to earn their blood money.

I swung around toward Billy but he was not there. The wounded Weldon was trying to drag himself clear of the fight and a rifle cracked behind me, scattering the gunmen but not before one of the standing dust-coated gunmen was blown clear off his feet by a double blast from beneath the saloon doors. At the same time, a prone Vargas belly down on the sidewalk entered the fray. The rifle again and another of Watts's hands dropped. I shot the man called Red Rivers in the back as he made for cover and, in the confusion of the noise and the black powder smoke, the man called Latigo made for the saloon only to be blown back out into the street by another blast from Vargas's scattergun. I had two rounds left, there was a scream from Bouchard as he took a bullet from one of the three remaining gunfighters. I did not hesitate; I shot one in the head and the other in the chest, dropped to one knee and ejected the empty shells and then reloaded on the run as I made a dash for the crippled back shot Rivers. He turned still in the fight, kicking at the gun in his hand, missing, losing my balance and rolling, turning and shooting him just above the left eye as he cocked the piece. The last of Billy Joe's men made the tethered mounts swung aboard and rode clear. Bouchard was down, the range too far for a shotgun and I was empty.

And as suddenly as it had begun it was over, sixty seconds of hell.

The tally: a wounded Bob Bouchard, six dead gunmen, a jubilant Vargas and a crippled John H. Weldon. So much for a few extra acres of prairie.

Of Billy Joe Watts there was no sign. Bouchard suggested that the young gunman may have been wounded in the sudden and bloody crossfire or that he finally saw that the odds of survival were stacked against him and he fled the scene like the coward he probably was. I knew better and that somewhere, sometime further down the line he would still be waiting for me, for the showdown he so desperately craved.

*   *   *

A couple of days later, Marshal Wally Dade arrived, accompanied by Sheriff Waxman. Dade placed the badly injured John Weldon under house arrest until such times as Doc Owens would OK his travelling back to Meridian where he would stand trial and, as Dade suspected, be released and ordered to keep the peace.

Waxman brought a deputy with him and installed him as the law in Carol Creek, releasing the old sheriff from duty. Lily Bouchard nursed her father through his days of pain from a busted leg, the bullet that downed him having shattered the thigh bone and leaving him with a permanent limp. She also persuaded him to return to Louisiana.

'We have many friends there, it is where we belong,' she confided in me shortly before the pair of them, along with Susan, left on the stage and the first leg of their long journey. 'Maybe Susan and I will open a café and get Dad set up in a general store. Anything is better than any more of his life spent wearing a badge.' She smiled archly at me, adding, 'You would always be welcome to visit if you are down that way.'

Bouchard for his part was more circumspect about the move, telling me it felt like a plan at the moment but he did not know how he would feel when he was over nursing the leg. 'You know something, Crow, I don't remember ever feeling that good, that rush out there on Main Street backing your play. Fanciful maybe, and maybe like the old time cowboy. We are men of the past, perhaps like him we are dinosaurs, men with guns and ideals that have long since died.'

I watched the coach to the end of the street, where it turned for the long trail to Meridian and beyond.

Dade shook my hand and wished me a safe ride back to Wyoming but I had one last chore to do and that meant a ride out to the Rocking J.

* * *

There was no one guarding the gate and the house looked deserted. I pulled the buggy up just short of the porch and waited. After a few moments Jimmy Keen appeared, held the head of the pulling horse and fed him some pony nuts before acknowledging me.

'The Weldons are not here. Mrs Weldon is visiting somewhere and the boss, as you know, is in town. You busted him up real good.'

'He didn't give me a lot of choice but that's not why I am here. I rode out to see you.'

'Me?'

'I want to buy a good riding horse, not a big animal but a friendly one.'

'We have such horses. Step down, main corral is out back.'

We walked in silence around the side of the building to the stables and the pole corral. Jack was there working leather and he grinned nervously at me. I nodded.

'No worries, Jack, I'm not packing today.'

Keen smiled and shook his head, leading me to the stable. I picked out a sturdy, pretty sorrel pony: good teeth, soft muzzle and friendly attitude. His legs were good and I figured him to be a sure enough animal. We argued over price as was the custom but settled on one we both thought to be fair and leading the pony back to the buggy, Keen asked, 'That for the kid, to replace the one Halloran shot from under you?'

I nodded and he handed me back my money with the bill of sale. 'That one is on the house, we owe it, consider it a debt paid.'

I did not argue the point, we shook hands, untied the pony and I climbed back up on to the buggy. 'Luck to you, Crow.'

'And to you, Jimmy.'

★　★　★

Luke was standing by the stable door when I got back. He took the reins and stared at the sorrel and then at me.

'The bay is saddled like you asked, Mr Crow, and your roll and war bag are tied on. We are going to miss you around here.' He looked again at the sorrel. 'What do you want me to do with the pony?'

'Take good care of him, give him a name, a good name, Ben might do it.' I handed him the bill of sale. 'He's yours, son.'

I saw the tears begin and gave him a hug so that he could hide them in my shoulder and for a brief moment I envied him his youth and the long trail he had ahead of him while mine was growing ever shorter. It was a momentary foolish thought and I let it slip away.

As I rode out of Carol Creek, lightning flashed, thunder close echoed around the valley and it began to pour with rain, and I had the sad feeling that I was leaving not a thing behind me that I would miss.

15

Homecoming

As keen as I was to see Laura Bainbridge again and to taste her summer wine, I did not hurry back to Wyoming. The bay and I made steady progress but I fished when the mood took me, stopped in the smaller townships for a soft bed and cooked food and other times hunted the foothills for my supper. I swam in the rivers and lakes and did all that I could to wash the stink of death and the black powder smoke from my body and my soul.

And finally there was that last hill and the ride down to the Circle B. The early morning sun was shining and a small herd of cattle were at the large water tank, the creaking windmill moving slowly in the warm breeze. Biff

Elliot, the old puncher, saw me and rode over, a wide grin on his grey bearded face.

'Hell, Charlie Crow, you sure are a sight for sore eyes and I am not talking about mine.'

I leaned over and shook his gloved hand. 'Everything OK here, Biff?'

'Sure will be now, boss has been watching this hill for the past week, hoping to see your dust. You had best get down there, we might be eating special tonight.' He slapped his leathered thigh. 'Or maybe not at all.' He wheeled his pony back to the cattle, chuckling to himself.

While hoping I still smelled sweet from my bath in Cheyenne Wells, I let the bay walk the last mile or so, then walked him into the yard and stepped down by the corral. I stripped the saddle, the blanket and my bags from the cantle and was about to remove my gun-belt when the hairs on the back of my neck stiffened much as they do on a dog or a coyote when an unseen yet perceived danger is present. In my business, it was not something to be ignored and I turned slowly to face the open stable door framing Billy Joe Watts.

'You took your damned good time getting here, Charlie, thought it would be today. We've been waiting all morning.'

I looked past him to the front porch of the ranch house where the last of his faceless dust-coated companions appeared. There was a rifle in his hands, held casually across his chest, walking clear of the flowerbed that decorated the front of the house.

'Do killers like that come by the bucketful these days, Billy Joe?'

'He's the last of them, Charlie, you and those damned lawmen back in Carol Creek done near cleaned me out.'

'Carol Creek is a long way from here, you follow me?'

'You left a forward mailing address with the hotel clerk, he gave it up easy.'

'Where is the woman?' I tried to sound casual.

'Your woman? She's OK for now, so is that old critter up on the hill all the time he keeps his nose out of this. The young puncher is in the barn with a sore head is all. This is just between you and me like it should have been back in Carol if that fool Weldon hadn't lost his head.'

'So what now? Who do I have to kill first, you or the pistolero?'

'You really think you are that good, Charlie, faster than me? Even if I let you pull first, you're a dead man and if by some act of good fortune, you do beat me then old Spence there will shoot you dead. It's just not your day.'

As he spoke, his shoulder dropped a fraction and he was fast, too fast. He had a sight picture of me in his head as he drew but I pulled and stepped to the left as I did so. His shot tugged my vest in passing and my round hit him hard in the chest. I was conscious of a roar behind me but I capped another round anyway before turning. The man called Spence was face down in the flower bed, the back of his head and his shredded hat covered in brain matter and blood with Laura Bainbridge standing behind him, calmly racking another round into the breach of the pump action shotgun in case it was needed. It wasn't; both men were down. Spence was dead and Billy Joe Watts dying. I nodded to her, holstered my gun, kicked Billy Joe's gun away from his hand, force of habit, and bent down beside him, cradling his head in my arm, wiping the flecked blood from his mouth and nose.

'You moved, Charlie, you damned well moved.' His voice was little more than a whisper.

'It didn't have to be this way, Billy, you should have let it be.'

'I'll be seeing you, Charlie, sometime, someday, somewhere further down the line.' His voice faded, that familiar expression of surprise lingering on his young face as the light in his pale blue eyes faded and he died there in my arms.

I laid his head down gently and walked over to Laura, carefully removing the shotgun from her hands. She was trembling. I put my arm around her shoulders and walked her back toward the house.

'Thank you,' I said, 'that's the second time you have saved my life.'

'Is it going to be all right, Charlie? Are there any more coming after you?'

'No, that's the end of it. Biff and I will clear up out here, you set a spell.' Suddenly there was a frantic raucous call as a large crow settled on the porch swing. 'That my rival?' I asked.

'Pretty much,' she said, her voice softening, her arm around my waist tightening. 'Some homecoming for you, eh, Charlie?'

A homecoming? I suppose it was and that word homecoming, it sounded just fine to me.

We do hope that you have enjoyed reading this large print book.

Did you know that all of our titles are available for purchase?

We publish a wide range of high quality large print books including:
Romances, Mysteries, Classics
General Fiction
Non Fiction and Westerns

Special interest titles available in large print are:
The Little Oxford Dictionary
Music Book, Song Book
Hymn Book, Service Book

Also available from us courtesy of Oxford University Press:
Young Readers' Dictionary
(large print edition)
Young Readers' Thesaurus
(large print edition)

For further information or a free brochure, please contact us at:
Ulverscroft Large Print Books Ltd.,
The Green, Bradgate Road, Anstey,
Leicester, LE7 7FU, England.
Tel: (00 44) 0116 236 4325
Fax: (00 44) 0116 234 0205

Other titles in the
Linford Western Library:

RED CANYON RED

Billy Hall

Some call her Red Kenyon the Red Canyon hellcat — and the young woman with an unmanageable tangle of red hair has proved herself the equal of most men on more than one occasion. But Red is only beginning to realize her mistake in trying to go after the stolen heifers alone. Far from any possibility of rescue, Leif Mortenson leers at the disarmed and helpless nemesis who has twice thwarted him. As panic and despair wash over her, Red knows she has the toughest fight of her life ahead . . .

SALOON

Owen G. Irons

Diane Kingsley, part-owner of the Cock's Crow Saloon, has made one too many enemies, and finally they've seen to it that she was thrown aboard a westbound train and sent out alone into the desert. Well . . . not quite alone, for, when she arrives, she finds that she has been riding with Walt Cassidy, who has also been run out of Sand Hill, for shooting the man who killed his horse. Walt is desperate — and intrigued by Diane's plan to build a saloon in an empty land . . .

GUNS OF SANTA CARMELITA

Hugh Martin

When former deputy town marshal Frank Calland helps out another saddle-tramp whom he finds stranded without food or water in the Arizona desert, he ends up being pursued by an angry posse — but this is only the beginning of his problems. He finds himself donning the lawman's star once more, this time as deputy to Marshal Bill Riggs, who seems to be hiding a dark secret from his past. Calland is thrown into the deep end, and must take responsibility when a band of ruthless outlaws arrives, blood-thirsty for revenge . . .